A PRODUCTION OF:

OWL BOOKS

* * * *

****

TOMORROW ELI

&

TOMORROW JANE

BY RYAN WOLDT

****

This book is for my father.
He has lived dramas I've only written about.
Dad, this one is for you.
I don't want hear any more complaints
that I never thank you
at the beginning of one of these books..
Thank you.

• TABLE OF CONTENTS •

01	Prologue
05	Chapter 1
10	Chapter 2
17	Chapter 3
22	Chapter 4
31	Chapter 5
37	Chapter 6
42	Chapter 7
52	Chapter 8
60	Chapter 9
67	Chapter 10
76	Chapter 11
84	Chapter 12
93	Chapter 13
101	Chapter 14
107	Chapter 15
113	Chapter 16
120	Chapter 17
124	Chapter 18
131	Chapter 19
136	Chapter 20
143	Epilogue
146	Acknowledgements

****

****

Prologue.

He leans on the wooden fence, looking out over the beach towards the ocean. From the cliffside boardwalk, he can see far beyond the last wooden pier. Small sets roll in. They appear as slight shadows on the surface of the water. Surfers jockey for position near the pylons. It is colder there under the darkness cast across the water by the Ferris wheel.

He shivers. This early, the sun only offers the illusion of warmth. *Small is better than nothing,* he thinks. *I should have gotten out here earlier.* He pulls open the hatch of the Prius and hangs his lightweight wetsuit off the roof rack. He wraps an oversized towel around his waist and kicks off his flips. Just as his shorts hit the ground, his phone rings, and he sees that it is her. He smiles.

"Hello, beautiful," he says.

"Ha! I don't feel beautiful," she replies. "Not right now."

"You are, though," he says.

"You're only saying that because you can't see me in this ridiculous pantsuit. I forgot what a pain in the ass it was to have to look like a professional," she replies. "And you haven't seen my hair yet."

"Did you do it? What do you think?" he asks.

"It's...it's a lot," she says. "I hope you like it."

"I'm sure I will," he replies.

"You better," she says.

He smiles at a man wearing a clown suit and holding a red nose walking past towards the pier. "I'm sure I will, but right now, I'm standing at the beach in just a towel. Can I call you later?"

"Sexy," she says. She leans over and frowns at herself in the rearview mirror. She brushes a loose strand of hair back behind her ear. "Can you drop me around the back of the building?"

"What," he asks.

"Not you," she says. "The driver. We're pulling up to the interview now. Just pick me up at three o'clock."

"You'll be ready to go that fast afterwards? There's no rush." he asks.

"I'll be ready," she says. "I brought clothes with me, and I'm leaving the pantsuit in a trashcan in the lobby."

"Ha ha! I'll see you soon," he says.

Click. The call disconnects. Jane looks at herself one more time in the mirror. *I wonder if I'd recognize me if I could somehow see myself as a passerby on the street might,* she thinks. "Thanks," she says and steps out of the car. The building is bright white with splashes of pink flowers setting off the path towards the entrance. A sign says, *No Smoking.* Another says, *No Dogs.* Yet another shouts, *No Skateboarding!*

Jane smooths out the fabric on the front of her thighs. For what feels like the millionth time, she checks her portfolio to make sure there are enough resumes for the group interview. There are, and she puts her hand out to pull open the door. *You can do this. You should do this. You can do this.*

Eli high-steps through the surf before pushing his board forward against the wave. He gently flops down on his chest and begins to paddle. The first waves he encounters aren't big enough to merit a duck dive. He goes up and over. Water slaps his cheeks. Another surfer cuts across a short face in front of him. They crouch low enough to drag their fingers against the surface of the wave.

"Yeww!" Eli hoots and paddles a little harder towards the horizon.

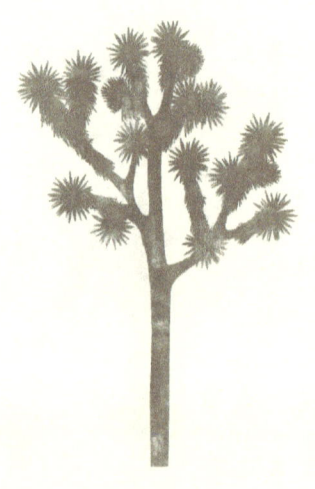

Chapter 1.

Eli

"Hey! Are you almost here?" Jane asks.

"Almost. Are you ready already?" I reply.

"Ready," she says, "but you need to hurry. Derrick is here."

"Oh boy. Will you be able to play nice?" I ask.

"I'll be the nicest," she says, and I laugh. "He's playing Elaine the new song he wrote for her in the living room."

"Derrick is the one with the bongos, right?" I ask.

"No, that was the other one. This one plays the didgeridoo," she replies.

"The didgeridoo? Really?" I say.

"Really. He never shuts up about studying abroad in Australia. He claims to be the Beyonce or Tay-Tay of the didgeridoo in America," she says.

"That sounds awful," I say.

"Oh, yeah, he's the worst, and he only orders flat whites at the coffee shop," she says.

"I'll be there in 45 minutes to save you, assuming the 110 doesn't get clogged in the next few moments. I'm just passing the South Bay Mall," I reply.

"You better hurry," Jane says, "or I'm breaking up with you."

"No, you won't. Then you'd be stuck with the Didgeri-dude all week instead of going out to the desert with me," I reply.

"Didgeri-dude. Nice one," she says.

"Thanks. I thought of it all by myself," I reply.

"Hey, Jane!" The shout echoes in Eli's ear.

"Hey, Harry!" Jane shouts back. "Sorry about that, Eli. What were you saying?"

"Just that I'd be there soon. Who was that?" I ask.

"Just Handsome Harry," she replies.

"Who?" I ask.

"Handsome Harry. You know that homeless guy that lives behind the sushi place? He's easily the handsomest homeless man I've ever seen. That long hair and tanned skin. He looks like he should be an actor," Jane says.

"Maybe he is. That would be a very L.A. story," I say.

"So totally L.A.," she replies. "So, see you in like 45 minutes?"

"Maybe less. Hopefully, less," I say.

"Good. My fingers are crossed for less. See you soon. Love you," she says.

"I love you, too," I say and smile. For the moment, good fortune is with me. The roadway is clear. I fly up the 110 past Gardena and Westmont. I split South L.A. and Alameda. The downtown skyline rises up on my left. I wrap around the old arena with the new name and the bank building. I exit onto the 101 and then again onto Glendale past the park. I turn onto Sunset Boulevard.

The lights catch me at Alvarado. I tap along in time with a Tom Petty song that pops up on my playlist. *I never really understood Tom Petty until I moved here,* I think. *Now, he's part of the landscape. Not bad for a Florida boy.*

The lights turn green, and onward I go. The late afternoon sun burns orange on the horizon. Its edges float and blur, disappearing behind hills only to surprise me over the next berm. I'm practically blind when the map app beeps and an arrow flashes. I blink the burn from my eyes and glance down at the phone propped precariously in the cup holder. It directs me left up the hill. *Soon, Jane. I'll be there soon.*

Jane

The sun reflects off the white stone of the church across the street. Spires appear in stark relief against the blue sky. Loud bass infused tones bleat from the organ inside. *Hurry, Eli,* I think. *Please hurry up.* I close my eyes, put my feet up on the rail, and lean back in the patio chair. I'm tilted just enough to sense danger. I take some deep breaths. *In. Out. In. Out. In—*

The door slams, shocking me out of my mini-meditation. The front legs of my chair drop to the deck with a thud. "Oh, you're still here?" says Derrick.

"Still here," I reply. *Shit. Be nice, Jane.*

"I thought you left already. I was just going to smoke, but I can go out back. Just warmer out here in the sun," he says.

"No worries. You can stay. Eli will be here soon, anyway," I say. *But maybe go around back.*

"Cool," he says.

Damn it.

Derrick pulls a baggie and some papers from his pocket. He plops down on the old wicker lounge with torn seat cushions pushed up against the far rail. I watch as he absent-mindedly but expertly begins to break the little nuggets onto the paper. When he finishes portioning, he runs the tip of his tongue across the edge of the paper and rolls a tight joint. He tucks it back behind his ear and begins the process over again. He lifts this one to his lips, where it dangles while he fishes around in his pockets for a lighter. "Got it!" he exclaims. He holds it up in the air like he is about to light the Olympic torch.

"Way to go," I say. "It looks like you're pretty good at that."

"I've got plenty of practice. I may be a science teacher by trade, but I was born to roll perfect joints," he replies. "You want a hit before I put my lips on it?"

"Your lips are already on it," I say, and Derrick laughs.

"Oh, yeah! This one, then," he says, reaching for the backup behind his ear. "It was for Elaine, but I can roll another."

I shake my head, hold back a sigh, and close my eyes again. *In. Out. In. Out.*

"You excited to head out to the desert?" Derrick asks. He doesn't wait for an answer. "I love it out there. We used to throw this huge party on the solstice. We'd have a dee-jay, a huge bonfire, lots of molly. We'd do it up big time! Not in Joshua Tree, where you're going, but some of the free BLM camping land nearby. It was crazy."

"Used to? Why'd you stop?" I ask. Derrick flicks his lighter in front of his face. He takes a big inhale off the joint. He opens his lips in a taut circle, letting some of the smoke out. It reaches towards the sky, but he sucks it back in with a pop before exhaling. The smoke particles hang in the rays of the sun for a moment before dissipating.

"Good question. I'm not sure, really," he replies. His lighter hand waves in the air. "Maybe we just got older. More tired. More responsibilities. Less willing to show up for work after three days of drinking and doing drugs and sleeping on the ground in the desert. Maybe."

"Seems reasonable," I reply.

"Mm-hmm," Derrick says. He takes another puff and waves at the youth pastor, opening the side door to the church across the street. The pastor frowns and rubs his beard but nods before greeting a few teenagers who've arrived early for youth group.

"I don't think he likes you," I say.

"He loves me," Derrick replies. "I still buy weed from him even though it is legal. My drug money has paid for a lot of nice white collars."

"Oh my gosh, really?" I ask. He nods and points down the walk.

"Eli's here," he says.

"Oh, thank god. "See ya later, Derrick." I grab my bags and head down the steps. Eli pulls up at the curb and reaches over to open my door. His hand cuts through a swathe of shadow, and like magic, the door swings open. I tuck myself down into the front seat.

"Holy shit," Eli says. "You look…just…holy shit."

"I know, right?" I reply. "Do you like it?"

"Wow, I'm, I'm, wow. It looks amazing. You look amazing," he says, and I smile.

"Thanks," I reply.

"Mm-hmm," he says.

"Hey," I say.

"Hey, yourself," he replies.

"You're staring," I say. Eli blinks and shakes his head.

"Sorry. Can you blame me? It's just…damn. It's so different, and, just…wow," he says.

"No, I guess I can't," I say and lean in to kiss him.

"Hey, Jane!" Derrick shouts. I twist back in my seat to look towards the porch. Elaine has come outside and wrapped herself around him. She leans over and takes a hit of the joint he's holding up in the air. His elbow is crooked and propped on his knee. She exhales the smoke. It floats out and up towards the heavens. "Happy Thanksgiving!" he says. Elaine waves with both hands. I wave, and we pull away from the curb.

Chapter 2.

Jane

"Look! Did you see it?" I ask.

"See what?" Eli replies.

"The sign. There is a taco stand ahead. Can we stop? Please?" I ask.

"We haven't even left L.A. yet," he says.

"I know, but I'm haaa-ngry, Eli," I say.

"Well, in that case, we better stop," he replies.

"My hero," I say.

"I'm not doing it for you. I'm doing it for me. I can't risk being stuck in the car with a hungry version of Jane. I might lose a limb," he says. I give him a look, and he laughs. "Don't be mad. You know it's true."

"The sign said the next left," I reply. The car slows, and the blinker goes *tick-tock, tick-tock.*

Eli

We follow the sporadic arrows with the taco graphics deeper than expected into the neighborhood. We're straddling a no man's land where the border of the city meets the ragged edges of the desert. We turn down an industrial street filled with concrete block buildings surrounded by chain link fences. It feels desolate. My throat starts to constrict. *Where is this place?* I wonder. Then, at the end of the block, I see it.

The sign on the overhang says, *TACO.* The letters must once have been a vibrant dark cherry but have since been worn by the sun and time. The 'S' has long since faded away. Over the order window, the menu has been hand-lettered in black paint. There are four options: Taco, Gigantic Taco, The Last Burrito on Earth, or Quesadilla Squared. A piece of paper taped to the window says, *Cash Only. No Change.*

"I'll have the Gigantic and a bottle of Coke," Jane says.

"A pair of tacos for me," I say.

"Chicken, beef, or neither," asks the woman behind the counter, and I answer. Her dark hair is held back with a net and red-checked bandana. She's wearing an old, oversized 49ers Super Bowl t-shirt. Caricatures of Joe Montana and Jerry Rice grin like clowns at the circus. Their jerseys are the same faded color as the sign above.

"$14.75," she says. I place a twenty on the counter. She smiles and adds the cash to the pouch tied around her waist. "No change," she says and disappears into the kitchen. A Spanish love song plays through tinny speakers somewhere above us.

"This feels like the kind of place where our food is either going to be the best ever made or send us to the hospital," I say. "If I had to guess, I'd say the latter."

"I know. I love it. I bet it will be great," replies Jane. She sits and leans back in a folding chair until her head just touches the wall of the taco stand. She folds her hands over her eyes, shading them from the setting sun, and smiles up at me. "Sit," she says, and I do.

I lean back, too. My chair scrapes the corrugated metal wall of the taco stand. I stretch out my legs. I let out a sigh and shut my eyes. Spots the color of 49er red dance on the back of my eyelids. When I open them, Jane is staring intently at me.

"Umm, what?" I ask.

"What are you thinking?" she asks.

"Right now? I'm hoping we don't get shanked because you wanted a taco," I say.

"Ha ha. Real funny. Seriously, Eli. Tell me something real. What's on your mind," she asks. The sun highlights the side of her face, and from my close angle, I have the odd sensation that I'm looking at her up on a movie screen. *So much bigger, brighter, and bolder than the reality of normal human beings. God, you are beautiful.*

"I was trying to figure out how I was going to convince the most beautiful girl in the world she should make out with me later," I say, and Jane smiles. *If I didn't know better, I'd think she almost blushed.*

"You're sweet, but you're insane," she says. "I'm not even the most beautiful girl at this taco stand."

"Not true!" I object.

"Very true. That woman back there probably has unlimited access to the homemade guacamole behind the counter. She wins hands down," Jane replies, and I laugh.

"You'd win in a fair fight," I reply. "I bet the guac comes in a 5-gallon bucket."

"Oh, that'd be amazing. *Buckets of guac* sounds like heaven," she says.

"Or a really good band name. Now, on the main stage, *BUCKETS OF GUAC!*" I reply. Jane snorts and laughs. "Guacamole buckets, or no, you're still the most beautiful woman at this taco stand, and all of Southern California, for that matter. No! The Americas!"

"Just The Americas? Not the world?" Jane asks.

"Well, I can't speak for some of the smaller islands in the Pacific. I'll need to do some research. I don't want to lose my credibility," I reply. I smile, and Jane gives my arm a light slap.

"You're crazy," she says.

Probably a little. "Probably true, but that doesn't mean I'm wrong," I say, and lean over to kiss her on the cheek. She turns, our lips touch, and everything goes a little blurry.

"Order up!" shouts the woman.

"Tacos!" whispers Jane, and I smile.

Jane

The Gigantic Taco comes out in its own metal holder that looks like it was originally designed for oversized manilla file folders. It stretches across a pizza tray, which catches a thick stream of dripping nacho cheese sauce. There are no tables, so I balance the monstrosity on my lap. *Precarious,* I think.

"Oh my god," says Eli, and I nod. "I've never seen anything like that. Ten bucks says you don't finish it."

"Calling it a Gigantic Taco is an understatement. It should be *the* Gigantic Taco, but challenge accepted," I reply, but I'm not confident I'll win. I examine the shell like a detective, looking for weak points in a suspect's story. I decide to start from above.

My first bite is mostly shell and lettuce. With my second, I've worked down to the tomato and guacamole and shredded cheddar. After a few more, I've dug so far down I can feel the rough edges of the crispy taco shell scraping my cheeks. I'm an explorer going further and further into a previously undiscovered taco trench. With my next chomp, I finally reach the seasoned meat. That's when I feel the tickle in my nose. I start to panic swallow but gulp in too much air. *Oh shit.*

The uncontrolled hiccup and the first of two sneezes—always two—meet somewhere in the ducts between my nose and throat. The force with which taco meat and cheese and lettuce exits my mouth is on par with a nuclear explosion.

"Ohhhh!" shouts Eli. It is a mistake on his part. I turn towards him as the second hiccup sneeze hits. I spray most of what is left of the partially masticated taco combined with saliva and snot all over his face and chest and lap.

"I'm so sorry," I say, or I try to. I'm still hiccuping, and Eli starts to laugh. When he really laughs, his eyes close, and his whole body shakes. It's infectious. I start to laugh, too. Then I hiccup again. A shred of cheese lands on my chin. Eli convulses even further into hysterics. We're losing it in front of the taco stand, and when the woman behind the counter steps out to see what all the commotion is about. It takes all of my effort to apologize again.

"I'm sorry," I reply, "I'm okay. I'm so sorry." She shakes her head and steps back inside. I look at Eli, and he smiles.

Eli

When Jane panics, her eyes get wide, and her nostrils flare. She starts reaching around with her hands but doesn't seem to know what to grab.

"Are you choking?" I ask, but she waves me away. Then, it happens in slow motion. Her body shakes. Her chest expands, and her shoulders draw back. Her head tilts, and her eyes close. Her neck snaps forward, and the hiccup and sneeze explode outward like a horizontal volcano.

"Ohhh!" I shout. The repercussions of my vocalization are immediate. *That was a mistake. Here it comes,* I think.

The crispier crumbs sting my skin as they impact my face. The nacho cheese is warm on my chest. The splatter sits thick on my shirt. Meat falls in clumps on my lap. Chunks of taco debris are scattered everywhere.

Tears and snot run down Jane's face. She's covered in food, and despite myself, I can't help but start to laugh. Then she starts to laugh, and I laugh harder yet.

"Can you still love me even though I spit taco all over you?" she asks.

"I don't know that I've ever loved you more," I reply.

"Kiss me?" she asks, and I do.

Jane

"You've got something on your cheek," he says. Eli reaches over and plucks a chunk of taco meat from my face. "I hope it's ground beef but it might be a hunk of lung."

"Oh my god, I'm crying!" I say. I wipe tears from my eyes. Another hiccup bursts forth from my mouth. Spittle flies, and we start to laugh all over again. We laugh until we can't anymore.

"Whooo," says Eli.

"Yeah," I reply. "Whooo." I release all the air from my lungs. I put my hands on my stomach and take a measured breath in hopes of preventing another onset of the hiccups. "My stomach actually hurts from laughing so hard."

"Mine too. Here," he replies and hands me some napkins.

"Thanks," I reply. "I'm so sorry about," I wave my hand in a circle around his chest, "all of that."

"I'll live," he says. "You know, I've always loved that you weren't afraid to eat in front of me. I feel like all the girls I dated before would only order salads to pick at. I always wondered if they went home and polished off a frozen pizza because they were so hungry."

"That's insane. I love eating. I think it's probably one of my three favorite things," I reply.

"What are the other two?" Eli asks.

"Probably sleeping and eating," I reply and smile.

"Eating twice?" he asks.

"I love it that much," I reply, "but maybe I'll drop the second eating further down the list."

"So that third spot on your favorites list is open?" he asks.

"For the right candidate," I reply, and Eli laughs.

Chapter 3.

Eli

The drive feels familiar. Strip malls have taken the place of roadside stands. Each is drabber than the one before until they give way to huffing chimneys pumping grey smoke into the sky. Boulders begin to stack on boulders as the highway gets wider and smaller and wider again. Little towns are tucked away just off the exit ramps. The buildings only borrow the land from the encroaching sand. The sun sets in my rearview until it all blurs together. My vision narrows. I see nothing but dust blowing over the blacktop and faded road lines—when there are road lines.

Jane's voice cuts through the whir of tires on the highway, wind through the cargo bars on the roof, and the bum, bum, bum-pah of the folk rock streaming through the stereo.

"When are we seeing Dana and her friends again? Will they be at the hotel tonight?" she asks.

"No," I reply. "We'll see them in a few days at Joshua Tree. It's hotel, hotel, camp, camp, camp, and then home," I say.

"Oh," Jane replies. "I didn't realize we'd be all by our lonesome in Palm Springs."

"I invited them, but I guess Dana still has to work tomorrow," I reply, "and besides, I didn't want to wait. I wanted to get you into a hot spring as fast as possible."

"You mean you wanted to get me into a bikini as fast as possible," Jane replies. I feel her grin before I see it.

"Maybe less than that," I say.

"Hey, now!" Jane exclaims.

I laugh. "Our hotel room has its own private patio with a hot tub. I wanted to surprise you with something nice," I say.

"Damn, Eli. Well done, but, um, do you have a plan for convincing me to leave all that luxury to go sleep in the desert? On the ground, no less?" she asks.

"Kicking and screaming if I have to," I reply. "Kicking and screaming." Now, it is my turn to grin. "Besides, we won't be on the ground. We'll be in the back of the car."

"Oh, well then," she replies.

"It will be fun," I say. "I promise. Dana always has a motley crew show up, and she is bringing her girlfriend, which is cool because we haven't met her yet. It's a different crowd every year, but, basically, it's anyone Dana knows that isn't doing a big family holiday event."

"What's her girlfriend's name again?" Jane asks.

"Umm…" I reply. *Shit,* I think.

"Eli!" Jane says.

"I know. I know," I reply. "I think it is Sarah or Cynthia or something. Something with an S-sound at the beginning, maybe? Dana will introduce her. I'm sure of it."

"Uh-huh," Jane says. She pulls her knees up into her chest. Her bare feet stick out off the edge of the passenger seat. I reach over and tuck a stay strand of hair back behind her hair.

"It's so bright," I say. "I haven't gotten used to it yet."

"I know," she replies. "Me neither." She nestles her cheek into my hand. It feels warm. I feel warm. The pulse in my thumb thump, thump, thumps. On the dash, my phone blinks, and the digital road turns red. "Watch out," she says. "Traffic ahead."

Jane

"It never really feels like you're going anywhere until you hit Riverside, does it?" I say. Eli pulls his hand away from my face and grunts in agreement as he turns his focus to the road ahead. Brake lights turn red, and he flips on the blinker to change lanes.

"Fucking Riverside," he says. "Always traffic. It is never-ending." He merges into the HOV lane and accelerates.

"Have you ever stopped? Is there anything to do here?" I ask.

"I always see a sign for this airplane museum. You can see some of the planes from the highway if you're coming from the other way. Old vintage military planes, I think," he says. "I've always thought about stopping, but I never do."

"We should go on the way back," I reply. "We'll make a good Riverside memory to hold on to. To help us survive future traffic jams."

"Okay," Eli says. He smiles. In profile, I see his one dimple raise slightly, and I smile too. His hair is cut short, and a slight sunglass tan cuts across his temple. The short hairs travel downward, covering his jawline. The darkness enhances the cut of his chin.

"Your scruff is thicker than normal," I say.

"I was trying to fit in," Eli replies. "Everyone had a beard up there. It's part of the Pacific Northwest uniform. See any grey or white hairs? I pulled one out near my chin the other day."

A small contingent of silver and grays have begun to amass around his ear. I close my eyes and try to imagine Eli as a silver fox, but it is just a bit beyond the grasp of my imagination.

"Portland was nice," Eli continues. "It kind of reminded me of when we visited your family. Lots of trees. Lots of trails and bicycles. Lots of beer. Way too many, actually. I wish you would have been there with me, though."

"Obviously," I reply.

"Actually, something cool did happen that I wanted to tell you about. We have so many projects, you know. I told the boss I needed some help. There is just too much for one person to do, and I kind of got a promotion, and—"

"Eli! That's amazing," I say.

"Yeah. It was nice to have all the work I've been doing recognized—even if I did have to bring it up to him. Anyway, he told me to set up some interviews and send him a pitch with what my new title and salary should be," he says. Eli glances over at me and grins.

"That's awesome!" I say. "I'm glad you finally said something."

"I know. I should have sooner, but—"

"But you're you," I interrupt.

"Yeah, but I'm me," he says and laughs. "I hope that's alright."

"It's alright," I say, and it is. *Almost everything about you is alright,* I think. I lean back into my seat and close my eyes. I see myself from earlier in the afternoon, forcing myself to smile and twisting my grandmother's ring around my thumb under the conference table. I twist the ring again now. The anxiety of remembering causes a visceral pain in my stomach. *Or maybe that was the taco. I wonder what Eli would say if I told him.*

I open my eyes to see the biggest concrete block building I've ever seen. "Oh my god!" I exclaim. "Is that a prison? It's huge." Endless walls extend into the desert. The grey stone bleeds into the dusk light and sand.

"Kind of. It's probably a warehouse or distribution center for some big box store, or it will be soon," he says. He squints. The hair at his temple dances. "It looks like the far end is still under construction."

"Like Amazon?" I ask.

"Sure," Eli says, "or any big retailer."

"Why's it so drab looking?" I ask.

"I don't think it matters too much to the workers inside," he replies.

"It looks like a really boring place to work," I say.

"Boring or not, it is keeping a lot of these little satellite communities on the map. Growing even, and probably for the first time in a long time, and...Nope, that is going to be an actual prison. I just saw a sign."

"Speaking of, I actually have some thoughts about work I want to talk over with you later," I say.

"Really?" Eli asks. "You didn't hear back from the interview already, did you?"

"No, it isn't that," I say, "but I want to get it right in my head first. It is too jumbled right now to share." In the distance, a hill rises to greet the sky. Bright beige boulders protrude from the mounds of dirt too small to be mountains but imposing nonetheless.

Chapter 4.

Eli

The car jolts as we exit the 10 to the 111 and onto North Palm Canyon Drive into downtown Palm Springs. It's already dark. By night, there is some leftover magic from old Hollywood. Shiny new buildings have been built up between the dark, old steakhouses on the main street. Some of the names over the storefronts have changed, as has the clientele, but the lit-up vintage neons found over the entryway awnings to some of the clubs, restaurants, and motels evoke hints of the glamour this town saw in its earlier years. Likely, there is more than a hint hidden behind the privacy walls of the boutique hotels.

"This is us," I say. The hacienda-style building is white, and the roof is comprised of stacked clay red tiles. Hidden lights on the ground illuminate the pathway. We follow a sage green rail along the stepping stones until we pass between two giant palms that set off an arched entry. The ornate iron gateway is already open. We step over the threshold and head down a hallway. Crushed velvet couches disappear into deep green walls textured by matching trellis accents and bookended by waxy-leafed palms in waist high pots. We cross under another archway and into the courtyard.

String lights with fat bulbs give off a warming glow. An old stone fountain flows purple, and the water drains down, emitting a comforting white noise. It mingles with music from a poolside cocktail bar that can't yet be seen but is definitely heard. The heads of two giant inflatable pink flamingos peek over the tall hedge lining the path. We continue until we come face to face with a stone Buddha. He sits cross-legged in our path. His existence forces us to choose—left or right. We follow the music until we reach a gap in the hedge, and Jane gasps.

"Oh my," she says. "It's so beautiful."

The pool is long and lit up from below. The inflatable flamingos have gathered near a wide stairwell, as if they were walking down into the water. More string lights crisscross above and extend over a section of the pool deck on the far end. A couple in all-white linens have made the space their dance floor. They sway to the thump of bass guitar coming through unseen speakers. A singer with a deep voice repeats, *"This is what I miss about the river. This is what I miss about the river. This is what I miss about the river."* The thump gets deeper. The voice gets faster, louder. More dancers emerge from the dark edges to gyrate and swivel in time.

Patio lounge chairs adorned with green and white striped towel rolls are aligned in perfect rows poolside. Tables and chairs near the building are illuminated by faux candles in hanging globes. The bar, a small half circle, juts out from the outer wall of the hotel. Open French doors lead us inside, where the other half of the circle looks out over plush green booths lining the outer edge of the room. Many are full. The early dinner crowd is already here enjoying the last of the posted happy hour specials.

Jane points at the passing dessert cart. Cherries tumble over the edge of a dark chocolate cake and cups of colorful whipped mousse capture our attention.

"Sir, Miss, may I take your bags to your room," asks a nattily dressed bellhop who has appeared at my elbow. I'm not sure where he came from.

"We haven't checked in yet," I say.

"I can take care of that for you, too, sir," he replies. He pulls out a tablet and begins typing. "Name?" I respond. "Got it," he says. His fingers swipe back and forth on the screen.

"Done. I see you are newcomers here. Is there anything else I can get for you before taking these bags for you?"

"I don't think so. Jane?" I ask. She shakes her head.

"Lovely, Paul here can get you a complimentary cocktail. I'll text you the room's QR code. It changes for every new guest," the bellhop says. Paul nods and smiles from behind the bar. "Thanks for choosing us. I hope you enjoy your stay here at The Wonderland."

"Thank you," I say, and watch as the stranger takes our luggage and heads out of the bar under yet another arched doorway.

"Cocktail, Jane?" I ask.

"Cocktail," she agrees, "and Eli."

"Yes, m'love?" I ask. I wrap an arm around her waist and pull her close.

"What is this place?" she asks.

"It's The Wonderland," I say.

"Wonderland," she whispers.

Jane

Eli and I sit at tall velvet-backed chairs, the same rich sage as the couches in the entryway and the booths and the stripes on the patio chair towels. The chairs rotate, and I catch my feet on the brass rail to bring me around to the glossy black bar top. It is so clean I can see my reflection in the sheen. The wispy blonde hair falling around my face is a shock.

Bartender Paul's white collar is precise. The cotton has been pressed. The top two buttons have been left undone. His beard is trimmed to create an angle near the chin that may not really be there. He has an easy smile, and the lines around his eyes bely his real age despite the youthfulness with which he commands the space behind the bar.

"Would you like a menu, or perhaps you'd let me choose the right cocktail for you?" Paul asks.

"That's a thing? Choosing for us?" I ask.

"I assure you it is a thing. I am pretty good at finding the right drink at the right time for the person or persons who've alighted before me," he says. "The question you have to ask yourself now is, do you trust the perception of the bartender, or at least, the magic of The Wonderland?" He grins and gestures towards the pool deck visible beyond the confines of the inner bar.

"Trust is a strong term," Eli says, "but in the spirit of The Wonderland…"

"Me too," I say. "Dealer's choice." Paul smiles and begins gathering ingredients. I turn to Eli. I rest my hand on the inside of his knee. "So—"

"I went a little overboard," Eli says.

"You went way overboard," I reply. My hand cradles his knee. I can feel his heat passing through the thin layer of cotton and penetrating my skin. I lean over and kiss his cheek. I put my hand behind his neck. I let my fingers crawl into the hair at the back of his head. I pull him towards me and whisper in his ear. "Way, way overboard."

"You haven't seen the room yet," he says.

"I can imagine," I reply.

"I'm not sure you can," he says. Eli's eyes squeeze tight the way they always do when he thinks he knows something I don't. "You look stunning."

"Don't I know it," I say and do my best to offer up a sly grin.

"And I wholeheartedly agree," says Bartender Paul. He clears his throat. "Stunning. The both of you. Here are your drinks. A classic Sidecar, a particular specialty of mine, for the lady, and a rye bourbon on a single ice cube with a twist of spiced Mandarin orange for the mister."

He sets the drinks down in front of us and offers up a little bow before stepping back and spinning around to take an order from the other side of the bar. I watch as Eli lifts his glass. Light reflects and prisms from palm and cactus-shaped engravings in the crystal.

"Oh. Oh, fuck yeah," says Eli.

"Good?" I ask.

"No, not good," he replies. "It's fucking perfect. How about yours?"

Beads of condensation roll slowly down the side, and the cocktail napkin sticks to the bottom of the glass as I pick it up. The fibers are rough and wet to the touch. Half the rim is sugared, and the granules break free as they brush against my lips. The drink is sweet yet dry. The liquor warms and leaves a pleasant fizzy burn on the tip of my tongue. My first sip finishes with a hint of lemon.

"Yep, fucking perfect," I say. With each sip, my body relaxes further into the chair.

"You are too kind," says Paul, who has returned from servicing other guests. "Please use those exact words if you find yourself relaying the story of this night to a compadre at some future time and place."

"What's in a Sidecar?" I ask.

"That one before you is brandy and Gran Marnier—to be particular—with a healthy squeeze of fresh lemon juice, and a lemon twist over ice. Depending on the guest, I might use bourbon or whiskey or cognac and orange, but for you, I chose brandy," he replies.

"May I ask why?" I ask. "I mean, why did you choose this for me?"

"Call it bartender's intuition and the vision of you two walking around the pool—bright and light and with the—"

He continues, but Eli's hand is traveling up my leg. I get lost for a moment. I smile at him, and he back at me. I give him a slight nod. "We should go," I whisper. "We should go now."

"–and that is why this was one of Frank and Marilyn and Sam and Dean's favorite places to stay when they were escaping the gossip writers of the time," Paul shares.

"Really? Wow. Well, Paul, umm, thank you for the drinks. They were—they are—perfect. Perhaps we'll be back later for a nightcap," says Eli.

"We'll be back for certain," I say. Paul doffs an imaginary cap.

Eli drops some cash on the bar and takes my hand. "Don't forget your cocktail, Jane. To the bungalow."

"The bungalow?" I ask.

"Our own corner of Wonderland," he replies, and off we go.

Eli

Soft lights under bushes and hanging candles illuminate the path to our room. Jane walks ahead, pointing out the pink flowers crawling along a balcony above, an outdoor fireplace in an alcove, and private walkways leading off to secret corners of the courtyard. She conjures visions of Rat Packers in skinny-leg suits sneaking off to smoke joints or engage in trysts with Hollywood starlets. All the visions are softened by the vaseline-coated glasses of time and shadow and imagination.

I walk behind, taking in all of Jane. *How did I get so lucky?* I think. *If I was on some other path that day, who knows where I would be now.* I'm brought to an abrupt stop when Jane's hand hits my chest. I push forward until my body comes to press against hers. She rests her forehead on my chin. I wrap my arms around her. The rim of her cocktail glass digs into my chest.

"Where were you?" she asks

"Lost in thought," I reply.

"About?" she asks.

"The turns of fate that brought us together on a deserted desert trail several hundred miles from here," I reply.

"That's all?" she asks, and I laugh.

"That's all," I reply.

"You were terrified of that snake. If I hadn't saved you, you would have likely died out there," Jane says.

"Oh, no doubt. I would have dehydrated like a stick of beef jerky and had a very sad obituary. Can't you see the headline? *Single man dies. Nothing left but bones and canvas shoes. Long dead rattler found nearby*," I reply. Jane giggles.

"That's too long for a headline. How about, *Single Man Dies in Desert!*" she says. "No, just, *Single Man Dies.* That's much more efficient."

"Jesus. That sounds so, so sad," I say. I hang my head, and she laughs.

"Can you believe it has already been more than a year? I still can't believe you gave me a ride that day," she says, "a complete stranger! What were you thinking?"

"Time passes when you're having fun. Besides, what else could I have done," I ask. "I couldn't leave you all alone in the desert, and, frankly, you were terrifying. I didn't know how to say no."

"I was?" she asks.

28

"You still are," I say. Jane's fingers climb my chest until her hands frame my face.

"How'd I get so lucky?" she asks.

"Are you reading my mind?" I reply. She kisses me. I close my eyes. Her fingers run through the hair on the back of my head. Mine curve around her waist and slide along her hips until she pulls away.

"I hope the room is close," she whispers. She bites her lower lip as she looks up at me. The candles fizz and dart. Everything blinks and blurs. The lights flicker and fade away.

Jane

"I think this is us," Eli says. He leads the way to the white door. It looks heavy and old. The knob is bronze. Green ivy has filled the space around the frame except where it has been cut away from a modern lockbox. "Do you have the code?" I ask. I wrap my hands around him from behind. Eli is fumbling with his phone.

"Right here," he says. He holds the phone up to the monitor, and with a click ker-chunk, the door unlocks. We push in, kissing and undressing as we go. Eli pulls my top up over my head. I start pulling on his belt and wiggling out of my jeans. He's laughing and kissing me, and I'm laughing and kissing him, and we're moving further into the room from the never-ending entryway. He grabs my hand and pulls me towards him.

"This way," he says and immediately trips over our bags. He sprawls face-first onto the runner rug leading into the suite. He yelps, and I giggle. I can't help it. He rolls onto his back. The giggles come harder. My stomach is shaking.

"Hey! Don't laugh. That hurt!" he exclaims.

I make my way until I'm standing over him with one foot planted on either side of his waist. "Will you live?" I ask. A breeze blows in through the open doorway. The air is cool on the back of my neck, and I feel tingles.

"Maybe," he replies.

I get down, my knees on either side of his chest. My hair drops down until it surrounds his head in a golden halo. "I think we're alone now," I say.

Eli smiles up at me. "I feel like we've been here before," he says.

"I hope you've got one more night in you, at least," I say. I lean in to kiss him before he can reply. His hands slide up my legs. I feel them squeeze as we breathe each other in. Eli kisses me back. I close my eyes and lean into him once more.

"Maybe one," he whispers.

Chapter 5.

Eli

"There's a full freaking bar in here! Whiskey, vodka, tequila, wine! They've got everything," Jane exclaims.

I smile and prop myself up in bed. The headboard is crushed violet velvet and soft against my skin. Jane wanders around the bungalow exploring. She flips a switch, and propane flames in the fireplace leap to attention. I fiddle with a remote, and music comes from hidden speakers.

"Holy shit, Eli. This place is like, whoa. Just whoa."

"Wait till you go onto the patio," I say. Jane slides open the door to what will temporarily be our backyard. Twinkle lights on short palms and along the privacy fence turn on automatically. They illuminate a swinging hammock, lounge area, and a tub filled with hot mineral waters piped in from a nearby spring.

"Fuck, Eli," Jane whispers. I can just see her curves in silhouette through the sheer curtain.

"Yes, Jane," I reply.

"This is insane," she says. She runs her hand over the surface. A ripple follows her fingertip. Jane steps over the edge of the tub and lets herself slide into the water. "Oh my god. It's the perfect temperature. Ohhh, yes. This is everything."

"So you like it?" I ask.

"Ahh, yeah. 'Like' is an understatement." she says. "I was right before. Bringing me here was a huge mistake."

"It was?" I ask.

"Uh-huh," she replies.

"Why's that?" I ask.

"There is no fucking way I'm going to want to go camping after this," she says, and I laugh. "Not only that, I may never even go home again. I'm moving here. I'll live in this bungalow forever and ever."

"And how would you manage to pay for the room?" I ask.

"I'll put it on your tab," she replies, and I laugh. "Or I could teach yoga and lead meditations to the other guests by the pool," she replies. "You could be the pool boy. I bet they'd give you some really short shorts—like really short."

"Seems reasonable," I reply, "but I'm not sure I have the thighs for the job."

"Come join me," Jane commands. I don't dare disobey. Away from the cushy confines of the bed, the air has a nip. I hustle up and slide into the other side of the tub. I dip down until my shoulders are fully submerged. My legs intertwine with Jane's. She squeezes my big toes. I run a hand under her knee and lean back. *The stars are out. So many stars,* I think.

"Hi," she says.

"Hi back," I reply.

"Remember when I said I had some work stuff before? There is something I'm mulling over," she says.

"Yeah," I reply. The stars twinkle.

"It was more of a work-life revelation," she says.

"Intrigued," I reply.

Jane

"I like your swimming suit," Eli says. He slides into the water and rests his head back on the lip of the tub. He spreads his arms wide, resting them on the rails.

"I'm not wearing a suit," I retort.

"That's probably why I like it so much," he says and smiles.

"Don't be so pleased with yourself," I say. I give a little flick of the water with my finger. The spray breaks through the steam rising above the rim of the tub. Eli leans forward to grab at my hand, and I flick at him again.

"I wish I could snap a photo of this moment," he says.

"Ugh, please don't," I reply.

"No camera, but I'm memorizing all the same," he says, "with my brain camera."

"Brain camera? Sounds suspect, but I'll allow it," I say. *How are your shoulders so perfectly square?* I wonder. I let my eyes wander around. I take in the curl of his hair, the thickness of his brows, the dividing line of his chest leading down into the water. He gives my calf a squeeze. *These are things I'll remember always.*

"Hi," I say.

"Hi back," he says.

Now. I should tell him now, I think. So I do. I tell him about my stomach dropping when I put on my interview outfit. I tell him how I sat in the conference room. I tell him I said all the right things. I smiled at the right time. I shook hands the right way. I tell him how the interviewer said, "I've got a good feeling about you." I tell him how when she did, I felt awash with an unexpected disappointment.

"I don't understand. They offered you the job, but you decided you didn't want it? Or they didn't offer it?" Eli asks. I shake my head.

"No offer yet, but I got a text earlier from one of my references that they already called her," I reply. "What I'm saying is, I don't think I'll want the job even if they do. I kind of want to make the decision before anything happens either way. So I know…"

"So you know it is yours. Your decision, I mean," Eli interjects. I nod.

"Something like that," I say.

"Are you sure this isn't a momentary fear?" he asks. "It is a big step, but you worked so hard to get the interview. You bought that classy new suit. It feels like you've been working towards going back into the corporate world for the whole last year."

"I know. I mean, I don't know," I reply, "but just today, I realized I'm an entirely different person now. Getting that job seemed like some sort of attempt to pick up where the old me left off before I left Chicago, before I came here, before I met you. You know?"

"I'm not sure I do," he says. He scratches the back of his head.

"It's like, I was on a pause—not with you but in my career, you know? Then, when I hit play, I wasn't sure I still wanted to watch the rest of that movie," I say. "I don't really know how to say it better than that." I'm trying to look Eli in the eye, but my eyes keep sliding off over his shoulder, over the fence, and upwards towards a few bright stars visible despite the lights of the city. *It's okay to be vulnerable, Jane. If not with Eli, then when? With who?*

"Does that make any sense?" I ask. "It would have been the right move for a past version of me, but this one... I don't know."

"Jane," Eli says. His fingers caress the skin just below my knee.

I blink, blink, blink, and turn until I'm once again meeting his gaze. He smiles, and I relax. *How does he do that? Make me feel so calm?* His eyes reflect the warm glow of the twinkle lights.

"It doesn't always have to make sense," he says. "Certainly not to me, and not even to you."

"It doesn't?" I ask.

34

"Not if it feels right. You're the one always teaching me about the connectedness of things and how our intentions guide us. So, no to the job. This job, at least. You can always change your mind."

"I can, can't I?" I reply, and he smiles.

"Do you have any idea what you are going to do?" he asks.

I turn the words over in my brain before saying them out loud for the first time. "Would it be insane to say that is what I want? What you just said? I want to teach people about the connectedness of things? I want to actually teach yoga and breathing and meditation. At least, I think I do," I reply. I feel a warmth growing in my belly. It spreads to my chest. It is a good kind of warmth.

"Insane? No. Surprising? Not really. Am I on board? Yes," says Eli. "You'd be great at it."

"Really? Just like that?" I ask. I'm surprised that I'm not surprised.

"Really," he says. "Just like that." He pulls me towards him. I don't resist. I roll around and slide into his lap. I lean my head back and kiss his neck.

"I haven't officially decided. I doubt they'll call before Monday if they even are going to make an offer, so I have a few days to think about it," I say.

"Mm-hmm," Eli replies. I feel his hands running along my ribs, curving around my hips, and exploring my thighs. "It sounds like the thinking part is already done."

"I don't know anything about starting a business or marketing. Is this just a really dumb idea?" I ask.

"No," he says. His hands come up my stomach and wrap back around my back. I feel him gently pushing me away, and I fall back into the deep curve on the other side of the tub.

Eli leans towards me. "You're smart, and you're strong, and if you want this, you should do it. I can help you."

"I wouldn't even wait if there wasn't this practical part of my brain shouting out, "What about rent! How will you ever retire! Be safe, you big idiot!" I say. "I mean, I don't want to live with Elaine and her Didgeri-dude forever."

"What if you moved in with me?" Eli asks. His eyes open wide.

"Holy shit! Really? Are you serious?" I exclaim. *I wonder if I look as surprised as he does.*

"Yeah, no kidding. Holy shit," he replies. He stands up in the tub. Water rolls off his hips, and he smiles down at me. "I think I need a drink."

"Me too," I agree, "Tequila, I think. Good tequila. If it's there in the bar." I watch him walk back to the room. *Holy shit.*

Chapter 6.

Eli

"So, are we really doing this?" she shouts from the tub.

"Do you want a chaser too?" I ask.

"Is there a lime?" Jane asks.

"There is a lime," I reply. *This place really has everything. Maybe we should move here,* I think. I pour the booze into a pair of glasses. They are real glass, not the normal shitty plastic-wrapped paper cups found in your average right off the exit hotels. I make a mental note to mention it to my boss. I cut the lime into quarters and add a little nick to the flesh. I grip the lip of the rim with the lime and make a full rotation. An acidic swath is left behind in its wake. I leave the sliced fruit hanging on the edge of the glass.

"Maybe bring the bottle," Jane shouts, and I smile.

I put it all on a serving tray and make my way back outside. I hand her the glass and drag over a lounge chair. I tighten the waistband of my hotel robe. It is white and made of a soft terry cloth that feels incredible against my bare skin. I take a sip. I think I contain most of my grimace. *It tastes like manhood and the tears of my enemies with a hint of sweet agave.*

"Is that your masculinity tingling," she asks. She smiles, so I know she's teasing.

"It was until you said, 'Tingling,'" I reply, and she smirks.

"Eli," she says.

"Yes, Jane," I reply.

"Is this real? I mean, was that a real ask? Not just an I'm looking at you naked on vacation ask? Like, you want me to move in with you? For real?" Jane asks.

Breathe in. Breathe out. Breathe in. Breathe out, I think. I feel the air pushing away the longer follicles of my beard and spinning off into the steamy condensation rising from Jane's shoulders. *This is a good thing, right? Moving forward.*

"Yes? I think so. Or maybe I could move in with you? Or, I mean, shit, do you even want to? Live together, I mean?" I ask. "You and me? In the same place?"

"I assumed you meant both of us, Eli," she says. Jane's gaze fixed on the sky far over my head.

What are you thinking, Jane?

"We're obviously not moving into my place," she continues. "There is a fifty-fifty chance Didgeri-dude ends up marrying Elaine, and she'd kick me out anyway. The real question is, do I want to?" I'm not sure if she's asking me or herself or one of the palms on the patio. She throws back her tequila. Her face contorts in the cute way it always does when she takes shots. She pulls the lime from the glass and bites down. Her face twists even more. She breathes out.

"Whoo! Fuck," she says. "Hey! No laughing at me!"

"Not laughing," I reply. "Remembering the last time we did tequila shots. At Duggan's place, remember? After the earthquake."

"I remember," she says, smiling. "To honor Mother Nature, or the Queen, or something. I remember throwing up the next morning, too."

"I was still asleep. I'm glad I missed that part," I say. "Who knows if we'd ever have gotten together if I had woken up a few moments earlier."

"Very funny. I wished I could have missed it," Jane replies.

"You didn't answer the question, though. Do you want to do this? If not my place, maybe a new place, a place that is ours," I say.

I let my hand drop down inside the tub. I break through the water and caress Jane's leg. She looks at me for a moment, then squeezes her eyes shut and slides down until her head is momentarily submerged. She breaks the tension on the surface like a submarine. Water pushes back and forward from her shoulders and drips from her ear lobes. She blinks her eyes open and uses her hands to rub the water away. Her hair, golden and wet, strings along her shoulders. A few strands run down her chest. I try not to stare. I try not to stare, but not very hard.

"Eli," she says. The pause is interminable.

"Jane," I reply. S*hit. This was a mistake. Just breathe. In. Out. Calm down. Shit. I should take it back and*—

"I really, really want to fucking move in with you," she says. She kisses my hand, and I smile.

Whoo!

Jane

I'm sitting on Eli's shoulders as he stands on a patio chair we've leaned up against the fence. I'm trying to see over into the next bungalow's yard, or I'm kind of trying to see over the fence. *I've had too much tequila again,* I think. *Way too much.*

"What do you see?" Eli asks.

This robe is amazing. So soft and—

"Jane!" Eli exclaims.

"What?" I reply. He weaves beneath me.

"Can you see anything?" he asks.

"No, but—" I say and pause to try to stop wobbling. I grip the top of Eli's head.

"Oww! But what?" he asks.

"I'm thinking about my robe. It's amazing," I reply. I run my thumb and forefinger along the seam running over my chest. "So warm. So soft. They're like, umm, like the high thread count of sheets, but of robes."

"Can you think about the robes and look at the same time?" Eli asks.

"No," I answer and continue to fondle my robe. "It feels like I'm getting a hug from a sheep."

"What?" Eli says and laughs. "Jane, will you please look over the fucking fence! I'm going to drop you."

"I'm looking! I'm looking," I say. I grab the top of the fence with my hands and lean over, staring. "I think they have two tubs! Wait, no. Now, it is just one. Wait! Two!"

"You're definitely drunk. C'mon, I'm letting you down," he says. The world shifts beneath me, and I'm flopped onto a chaise lounge.

"Oof!" It's more of an exhortation than an actual word. "No, I'm not," I say. "I'm just sort of drunk." I blink, blink, trying to focus on the stars or an umbrella or the palm leaves that break into the frame of my sight. It isn't working. *I'm really drank—no drinked. Shit. Drunked. Definitely drunk.*

"I know a buzzed-up Jane when I see her," Eli says. He lies down on the ground beside my lounger. I drop my hand over the edge. Eli's fingers wrap around mine. For the moment, we both stay quiet, staring up at the sky. The world expands and contracts at the edges. The stars split and combine, and I can feel the leftover burn from the booze in my throat.

"Do you still lovvvveeer me?" I ask. "Even though I'm drunky, drunky?"

"Still," he says.

"Eli," I say.

"Yes, m'love," he replies.

"You think you're ready to live with all this? I mean, really ready?" I let go of his hand to make a sweeping TV gameshow host gesture towards myself.

"I'm ready, Jane. I've met your parents. You've met my mom. We say *I love you*, and you're already at my place half the time, more than half. The next big step is moving in, right?" he replies.

"That's imperv, umm, impervious timeline logic. Fives?" I ask. I raise my hand high overhead. Eli slaps it five. Then he takes it and holds on. His thumb runs along my lifeline. He presses into my palm. This time, my fingers close around his. *How many more big steps are there?*

"I think I'm going to have one more drink. You want one?" he asks.

I want one.

"I want one, but that probably isn't a good idea. There are two Dippers in the sky right now," I reply. He laughs and squeezes my hand.

"There are always two Dippers, hon. The Big and the Little," he replies.

"Wait, what? Really?" I ask. "How did I not know that? I knew that, didn't I?"

Eli pushes himself off the ground. "Oof," he says, and I laugh. "Really. Always two."

"That's amaze—hiccup—amazing," I reply.

"Did you just say hiccup out loud?" he asks.

"You know what? What's one more?" I say.

"I'll make it with a lot of ice," he replies.

"Adulting!" I say. I hiccup, and we laugh.

Chapter 7.

Eli

"Be right back, love," I say. I brush the hair from her face. I lean in close to give her a kiss on the cheek. She turns into me, catching me in an embrace. She slides under the crook of my shoulder. Jane moves her hand down along my torso until it settles on the curve of my hip.

"Stay," she says. Her eyes stay closed. I smile.

"If I stay," I whisper, "neither of us will get coffee this morning."

"Go. Go quickly!" she replies, and I laugh. I kiss her and break free from her half-hearted attempt to keep me close.

There is already a hum of energy emanating from the pool deck as I pass. The sun isn't overhead yet, but if the first rays are any sort of warning, *"It's gonna be a hot one." My mom always said that,* I think.

I'm sure the shop's name is somewhere above the rust colored overhang, but I don't see it. The sign I do see says *COFFEE* in san-serif letters lined up vertically on the door. They break into the reflection of a palm tree backed by the endless blue sky. I push, and then I pull. A bell jingles my arrival as I cross the threshold. The chill of air conditioning blasts into my face.

"Welcome to Coot Coffee!" says a voice. The mouth it emanated from appears in the form of a heavily tattooed barista. She steps around the corner. Her hair is jet black with wisps of silver wrapping around her face. Her black leggings are torn. A black t-shirt is tied up at the navel, and her sleeveless jean jacket is covered in pins and patches. One over her chest features a grim reaper holding a coffee pot. It says, *I like my coffee black like my soul.* Another on the arm has a skull and crossbones. The words *Death Before Decaf* come from its wide-open jaw.

"Hi," I say. My voice cracks. *Dry from the desert air and probably all the shots, too much tequila. At this point in my life, I should know better.*

"Hiya, yourself," the barista replies. She leans on the counter, and her short sleeves ride up her arms. Black ink across her bicep reads *Heartbreaker* in cursive."You look like you could use a coffee or two."

"Maybe three," I retort, and she grins.

"A good night calls for a good morning," she says.

"How'd you know?" I ask.

"The bloodshot eyes give you away," she replies. It's my turn to grin, and I do. I think I do. It aches to move the muscles in my face.

"Can I get a dirty chai latte and a black drip coffee to go and an espresso for here?" I ask.

"You can. You may, and you will. Name?" she asks.

"Name of what," I reply.

"You," she says.

I look around at the empty cafe. "Eli," I say.

"Nice to meet you, Eli. I'm Willa," she says.

"You too," I reply, only to be drowned out by the grating of coffee beans being ground. While I wait, I try to focus on the room, if only to stave off the looming nausea. The menu board on the wall looks custom-built. The red grain stain reflects the warm light from a modern hanging chandelier. Two walls are smooth, natural grey concrete. The third is wallpapered with the repeating pattern of a black duck-like bird with a blood-red swath ringing the pupil. The last has floor-to-ceiling shelves covered in all sorts of Coot Coffee branded merchandise—mugs, shoulder bags, sweatshirts, and dad hats—featuring the red-rimmed stare from a psychotic duck.

"Espresso first," Willa says, setting down a saucer. The small demitasse glass is filled three-quarters full with a shot of coffee. Tiny bubbles form a velvety smooth crema. "You look like you're from L.A."

"What does someone from L.A. look like?" I ask.

"They look like you," she replies. She points at my chest and laughs. Block lettering on the inside of her wrist reads *Savage*.

I laugh. I try to laugh. It sounds forced. My throat cracks again, causing me to cough. I take a sip of the espresso to wet my throat. "Hey! That's pretty good," I say.

"I know. Just the right amount of the darkness. The bitterness offsets the sweet. We roast it ourselves," she says. Her hands are readying my takeaway coffee, but she holds eye contact with me. "I was right, wasn't I? L.A.?"

"Close. Long Beach," I reply.

"Same, same," she says. "It's all L.A. to me."

I nod. "I guess I'm from there now. Not originally. How'd you guess?" I ask.

"It wasn't a big leap. I didn't recognize you, and I know most of the locals that come here. It seems like half of the city comes out to the desert over Thanksgiving," she says.

"You must hate all of us interlopers," I reply.

"Nah, tips get better for a few days, but I do wonder why you come. Don't any of you have family dinners?" she asks.

"We're out here searching for something, maybe?" I reply. "Something bigger than family dinner, I guess."

"That must be why the nightclubs are all packed until the wee hours of the morning," she replies.

"Late night activities are part of the search," I say.

"Ha! A bunch of vampires, more likely," she says.

"Yep. We're all vampires just out here, umm, vampire-ing," I reply. "This is our annual convention. We come out here the same week every year."

"That makes a lot of sense. Palm Springs is perfect for vampires," she says and smiles. She brushes her hair back, exposing a half-dozen tiny silver hoops wrapping around her upper ear and another tattoo, a sliver of the moon, inside the upper lobe.

"Maybe we like it out here in the desert because it feels like it is just on the edge of desolation. We are packed in so tightly along the coast, you know. Yet somehow, we're still isolated by highways and Hollywood."

Willa rolls her eyes. "I feel terrible for your plight," she says, and I laugh.

"At least out here, we can pretend we're isolated by design," I reply. "To us, Palm Springs is the edge of the wilderness."

"Where the dinosaurs once trod, and sundown comes with endless dangers," she replies as she sets two tall cups on the counter. "But with hot springs pools and never-ending drink service."

I laugh and nod. "Something like that," I reply. I take a sip of the espresso. It is creamy and rich with just a hint of saltiness. I slurp the rest down in one go. Willa wipes down the countertop and takes away the miniature cup and saucer. "So what's a coot?" I ask.

"It's that bird on the wall. The one with the black feathers and fucked up red eyes," she says. "I've never seen one, but they say they're common around here, and since our owners are a pair of crotchety old dudes, the name works two ways."

"You're funny," I say.

"You're cute," she says.

"I have a girlfriend," I reply. "We're moving in together, I think."

"You ordered a dirty chai latte to-go. I would've guessed there was a girlfriend or boyfriend somewhere," she replies.

Savage.

The door jingles again, and a whirlwind zooms past me.

"Mom!"

Willa smiles down at and then embraces the little boy who's attached himself to her legs. He's rocking kids' checkered slip-on Vans, jeans, and a Johnny Cash t-shirt. "Hey, kiddo. Where's your Dad?" she asks.

"He's, he's, umm, outside, but Mom, guess what?"

I glance out the door to see a man in a matching, albeit adult-sized, Johnny Cash tee leaning up against an old truck, talking on the phone.

"I'll guess in just a moment, hon," Willa says to her son. She reaches down and pulls him into her legs for a hug. "Sorry about that, L.A. That will be $13, but for you, $13 plus tip."

"No need to apologize. Cute kid," I reply.

"Yeah, we did alright," she says and smiles. "See ya later, vampire."

I glance back over my shoulder as I cross the threshold into the world again. Willa gives a little wave. She says something to her kid, and he waves, too. The man by the truck gives me a nod as men do when they pass on the street. I look at the two palm trees towering overhead. They lean ever so slightly in the breeze. They beckon me forward. I pass between them and under the arch back into The Wonderland.

Jane

The lounge chairs at the pool are nearly full despite the early hour. Servers are handing out mimosas, and a couple of couples with pre-teens on their shoulders are already playing chicken in the water. I claim a pair of lounge chairs tucked as far away from the speakers as possible. The music isn't bad—Ray Charles, The Pointer Sisters, Nina Simone—just loud. *It's the kind of music my parents always listened to when I was a kid,* I think. *It's the soundtrack to a nostalgic kind of movie.*

I conjure up a memory of them putting a record on. I hear the click of the player's arm as it rotates over and across the spinning disc. The needle drops down with the slightest scratch. I feel my brother's presence kneeling beside me. It is dark at the edges, but there in the middle of my memory is Dad taking Mom into his arms and spinning across the room.

I smile and try to hold onto the scene, but my head starts to throb. *I wonder where that record player went? Maybe Dad still has it.*

I roll out the striped towel lengthwise on the cushion. A light breeze cuts across the pool, prompting goosebumps on the skin around my navel and along the tops of my thighs. I steal Eli's towel to use as a light blanket until the mid-day heat fully arrives. I close my eyes until a shadow causes me to shiver once again.

"Mimosa, miss?" asks the waiter. He's wearing a short-sleeved collared shirt that is tight around his biceps. It is unbuttoned at the neck and tucked into a pair of crisp khaki shorts. The fabric barely extends below his service apron. *Is he wearing that mustache ironically or committed to the look?*

"Mimosa? I haven't even had coffee yet," I say.

"No judgments, miss," he says. When he grins, perfect channels are created in the folds of his cheeks.

"Feel free to judge away. Two, please. One's for my boyfriend. He went to get coffee but will be here soon," I reply. "We're in room—"

"You're good," he interrupts. "First round poolside each morning is complimentary for Wonderland guests."

"In that case, make it four," I say, "and a Bloody Mary."

"Good call, miss. It's important to have your fruit and veggies in the early part of the day," he replies. I don't think he is joking. His mustache wiggles when he talks. It pulls up under his nose when he smiles. His cheeks redden around his dimples.

"When in Palm Springs," I say. *Whatever that means.* Then, he's off to the next set of occupied loungers.

Somehow, you're pulling that look off, young man, and free drinks? This place is ridiculous. The couples playing chicken in the pool have moved on to inflatable flamingo races. The kids ride the bulbous birds like chariots. The kicking and paddling are furious, and it appears that a few other guests have begun gambling on the action. I lean back and adjust my floppy hat to cover my face from the sun, which seems to be magnifying itself on my skin, even though the air around me is still brisk.

"Your breakfast beverages, miss," says the server, "and a food menu for you to peruse at your leisure. I recommend the eggs Benedict. They are a locally known classic." He sets down a drink tray, and begins to walk away.

"Wait!" I say. "Can I order food right away?" He does an abrupt-about face.

"Certainly," he says. He puts his hands behind his back and looks down at me.

"Won't you need to write it down?" I ask.

"I've got it," he says and taps a finger to his temple.

"Alright, but it's gonna be a lot," I say while skimming the menu. "No Benedict for me. I don't like that gravy that comes on it, but I'll have the French toast and the egg scramble with goat cheese and sausage. Can I add bacon to that?"

"Certainly, miss," he replies. His mustache quivers ever so slightly.

"Great. Then add one of these toasted everything bagels with cream cheese and an extra side of bacon, please. Oh, and home fries! With ketchup," I say.

"Is that another extra side of bacon, or just the one coming with the egg scramble," he asks.

"Another," I say, and the quiver in his mustache turns into a full grin.

"Will that be all?" he asks.

"For now," I reply and smile. He nods and turns to go but stops. He turns back. His mustache twitches.

"Yes? What is it? Do I need to choose another side, or?" I ask. He shakes his head.

"I must say, miss, that was a helluva order. Quite impressive," he says. "I appreciate a woman who's willing to eat a real meal. I felt compelled to say so."

"Well, I do declare," I reply and press my hand against my chest just below my chin. "Is that so rare?"

"I think we're still within the swirling vortex of Los Angeles, so, ahh, yea, miss. Very rare," says the waiter.

I'm going to call him Mustache Max. "My boyfriend will probably eat some, too," I reply.

"Probably?" he asks.

"Maybe," I say. "If there is any left when he gets here. Can I add something to that order? A jug of water? And a refill on this?" I ask. I drain the nearest mimosa, bite into the juicy flesh of the perfect half-round of an orange slice, and hand him the champagne glass.

"Certainly," he says, and I smile. He leaves, and I take a moment to let my eyes wander. Tables and chairs have been set up near the bar for breakfast diners. Fresh-cut flowers serve as centerpieces. Umbrellas along the pool deck provide shade. At the far side of the courtyard, private lounges are separated from the rest of us by flowing white cotton curtains.

I look around at the collective of people laughing over their egg scrambles or reading magazines in the sun. There is splashing in the pool, where the races have devolved into a cannonball competition between brothers and sisters and moms and dads. Waiters deliver mimosas. *Real life is for whatever is happening outside these walls. It is all smiles at The Wonderland.*

I see Eli first. He stands near the fountain at the entry to the courtyard. He is on his tiptoes, stretching beyond his full height to scan the pool area. He blocks the sun from his eyes with a hand. Even from this distance, I can tell he's squinting. When he finally spots me, I wave, and he smiles.

"Can I interest you in a dirty chai latte, beautiful?" he says.

"My hero," I reply. I reach for the cup, but Eli pulls it back.

"That will be $7.50," he says. "Special pricing for the beautiful lady."

"Oh shit. I don't have any money on me," I reply, "but if you give me that coffee…" The sun's rays directly behind Eli's head give him a surreal, blown-out halo.

"If I give you this coffee, what?" he asks.

"I'll let you see under this towel," I reply, flicking the edge of the towel up and down. *I'm so obnoxious. Why does he love me?*

"Fair trade!" Eli exclaims and thrusts the latte towards me. I start to laugh, but he interrupts me with a kiss.

"Why do you love me?" I whisper.

"How could I not?" he replies. "Now let me under this towel!"

I laugh, and Eli laughs. There is a splash, and someone on the other side of the pool shouts, "Cannonball!"

Chapter 8.

Jane

The music gets louder after dinner. The bar lights get lower. My skin is crisp from a long day of napping by the pool. *The sun sets so early,* I think.

Another button has come undone on Bartender Paul's shirt tonight. The poolside tables are filled with hipster-looking men and women from a wide range of generations. A few well-dressed old-timers argue next to us at the bar. *Is that a cashmere cardigan?*

"Why, one night, Sammy Davis Jr. played that piano right over there!"

"No! You're remembering wrong. Sammy danced on it."

"Right there on the piano!"

"No, it was Frank's guy—that handsome young man—that played, and his kid, Sinatra's kid, who sang!"

"Nancy? No, that's not right, Arthur! Sammy played, and Sinatra and Nancy sang. You remember, don't you, Clyde? Clyde?"

"What?"

"I said Sammy played. Frank and his kid Nancy sang. Remember that?"

"No, no, no! It was Sammy that played. Nancy danced. Frank and Judy sang. Remember, because Dean sat with us for a spell?"

"He bought us a round!"

"Who bought us a round?"

"Two rounds!"

"That's right. He sure did, Milt! Scotch whiskey and sodas, I think."

"That Dino was a heck of a guy!"

"Helluva guy."

Paul comes by to get our drink order. "Something new tonight? Or the same as last night?" he asks, and Eli answers for us both.

"The same, please," he says. I lean over to the nearest of the arguing senior citizens.

"Excuse me. Milt, is it? Did Sammy Davis Jr. really play here? Or Sinatra or any of the Rat Pack?" I ask. "Or are those just stories?"

"Sure he did. They all did! They played that piano right over there in the corner," he replies. They played and sang and danced all over this room."

"That was before they renovated," says the one called Clyde. "When this place was still The Inn at The Springs."

"That's right," confirms Arthur. "Lots of wood paneling and a fireplace over there. You could still smoke in here back then." The other men nod.

"That's amazing but, I have to ask, why is that piano still sitting in that corner? Shouldn't it be in a museum or something?" I ask.

"Museum? If they put every piano one of those gents played or sang next to in this town into a museum, well, that'd be way too many pianos in museums," Milt says with a chuckle.

"They'd have to build a museum just for pianos!" says Arthur.

"It belongs on the trash heap," says Paul as he sets down our cocktails.

"Trash heap? Really?" says Eli.

"Really. It hasn't been tuned in years, and half the keys are broken, but the owners think like you. They keep it as a nod to the history of this place," he replies. "There is a little plaque on the bench."

"That seems so sad," I say.

"So much history is piled up over at the Westside dump," says Clyde.

"Ain't that the truth," says Milt. "You know, rumor is that Sammy got into a knife fight right out there in the parking lot." He points towards the nearest exit.

"No way," says Eli.

"It's true," Milt continues. "They stitched him up in Dino's suite, and he came back down here to play another set. Chain smoked and drank gin and tonics the whole time."

"That's not true. There is no way it's true," I reply.

"As true as an honest man's arrow," replies Milt, "and —"

"Ahh, quit joshing the kids," says Arthur. "That never happened, and you know it!"

"I'm not joshing anyone," says Milt. "That's as true a story as any you've ever told, you wrinkled old mango!"

I laugh and take a sip of my Sidecar. *It's perfect.* I catch Paul's eye, put my hands together in a namaste pose, and give him a little nod. My thumbs press into my breastbone. I take a deep breath. My chest expands and contracts, and I'm reminded that we're all connected. *Me, Milt, Eli, Judy Garland, and Sammy Davis Jr. are all one in the through line of history. We're existing in the same space. We're breathing the same air but at different points in the timeline. Perfect.*

I run my hand down Eli's leg until it rests just inside the knee. He blushes. I sip my drink through the thin, red straw. The music has gotten even deeper. The thump of the bass reverberates through our shoes. Out near the pool, I see people starting to dance under the twinkle lights strung up over the makeshift dance floor.

"What are you smiling at goofball?" Eli asks.

"Will you dance with me," I ask.

"Ahh, shit. Jane, I don't, I mean, you know I'm a terrible dancer," he replies. He visibly stiffens up, but I don't care. The twinkle lights reflect off the pool. I lick a few grains of sugar from my lips. The sweetness of the Sidecar lingers.

"Dance with me," I say. "Please."

"Jane, I—" Eli says, but Clyde reaches over. He sets his hand on the bar and snaps his fingers to get our attention.

"Son, when a beautiful woman asks you to dance, you dance," he says. Milt and Arthur nod vigorously behind him.

"Or a beautiful man," interjects Paul.

"Ain't that the truth," says Milt again.

"But—" says Eli.

"No buts about it, kid. Me and Artie—he's the one on the end over there—have been together for 45 years. Trust me on this," says Clyde.

Eli puts his hand on my hand. He gives Clyde and the boys a nod. He intertwines his fingers with mine. He smiles as he looks up at me.

"Jane," he says.

"Eli," I reply.

"I would love to dance with you," he says, and I smile.

Eli

I think Jane is leading, but I'm not entirely sure. My body is moving—sometimes faster and sometimes slower. I'm not in control of where it is going or when. Jane is laughing and smiling. The beat slows down, and she throws her arms around me. She nuzzles her face into my neck. I feel her lips press against my skin. I feel her body flush against mine. I hear her voice, and I feel warm.

"I'm really happy," she whispers, "right now, today, and I can't wait to move in with you."

"Me too," I whisper back, "to both things."

We're swaying near the pool, and we're not alone. The pool deck is full of partners moving, mostly in time, to the sounds emanating from the speakers. Bodies list and lilt around us—back and forth, back and forth—like off-kilter metronomes. The string lights twinkle like stars so close we can almost touch them, and the steam from the pool completes the cinematic scene. *It feels like anything can happen,* I think. The old man named Clyde gives me a thumbs up from the bar.

"Look," Jane says. She turns our bodies so I can see down to the far end of the pool. Another couple sways to the music. Between them, a little girl stands on the man's feet and hangs onto his knees. "That might be the cutest thing I've ever seen."

"Mm-hmm," I say. "How old do you think they are?" *I wonder if I'd be that cool of a dad?*

"The kid or the couple?" Jane asks.

"Both," I reply.

"I'd guess the kid is like three, maybe four, and the couple, umm, I don't know. I'm terrible at this game. Younger than us. Late twenties, I'd say, if I had to guess," she says.

"That's about my guess, too," I reply. The little girl falls off her dad's feet and is swooped up into her mother's arms. The little girl giggles and shrieks as she's tossed into the air. Jane gives me a squeeze.

"You okay?" she asks, and I nod.

"You?" I ask. She nods. For the moment, we sway in silence. Side-to-side. Side-to-side.

"Hey," I say.

"Hey, back," she says.

"How about we grab another drink, head to the room, and watch a movie?" I ask.

"Is that what you want?" she asks.

"That's what I want," I reply. "As long as it is what you want, too."

"That sounds good, but only, and I'm serious about this, only if you follow the rules," she replies.

"What rules are those?" I ask. "I didn't know we had rules."

"We didn't. I'm making them up as I go," Jane says, and I laugh. "Promise me, Eli. Promise you'll follow my— admittedly arbitrary—rules."

"It seems dangerous, but I promise," I say. I hold her tight. We're one entity swaying back and forth on a concrete dance floor under the desert sky. Overhead heat lamps, pool steam, and Jane pressed against my chest keep me warm despite the cool wind slipping over the walls and pushing through the courtyard. "I'm ready. What are the rules," I ask.

"Rule one—are you ready for this?" she asks. I nod again. "Okay, first rule is we have to order two rounds of drinks at the bar. No! Two rounds each! I know we can make our own in the room, but these Sidecars, Eli, oh my god. They are so good. Paul may be a legit genius. Between the two of us, I think we can carry four."

"Seems reasonable," I reply. "What's the next one."

"This one is more fun," she says. She smiles up at me. I run my hands along her arms, down past her shoulders. I caress her ribs. I let my palms settle just above her hips. "The second rule is–drumroll, please." I tap out a beat on her lower back. "No pants while we watch the movie. In fact, no pants in the room for the rest of the trip. That is my second rule, and it is non-negotiable." She squeezes me, and I laugh.

"It sounds doable," I say. "Pants are the worst. I've never really liked them."

"You sound doable," she says. She laughs at her own joke.

"Right back at'cha, babe," I say. "To the bar."

"Wait! You haven't heard my third rule yet," Jane says.

"There is a third?" I ask.

"I'm pretty sure I said three," she says. She grabs my hand to pull me back. I take the opportunity to envelop her with my arms and kiss her lips. She smiles and looks up at me. *Uh-oh. That's her mischievous smile.* "The third rule is more of a dare."

"What is it?" I ask.

"You promise you'll do it?" she asks.

"Promise," I reply. *I don't know that I could refuse you if I wanted to.* "What is it?

"Where is your phone?" she asks.

"My phone? Why—"

"Eli!" she says.

"Sorry! Sorry. It is in my coat over on the chair by the bar," I reply.

"Good. I dare you to jump in the pool with me," she says. She grins.

"What? Jane that is—" I start to reply, but she takes my hand.

"Ready, Eli! On three. One! Two!" she says.

"Jane! I—" I try to interrupt but fail.

"Three!" she shouts and leaps. She pulls me with her. It isn't a jump, but my body falls forward through space. Jane lets go, and my arms flail through the air. The splash is loud and obnoxious. I bob up to hear Jane laughing, and I'm laughing, or I'm trying to laugh as I cough and spit out a mouthful of pool water.

There is another splash, a shout, a laugh, and a splash, splash as more once swaying bodies land in the heated water. Plumes of pool water are sent skyward. Gravity claws them back to earth. The droplets rain down on our heads. I grab for Jane's hand and lean back to float. The stars twinkle, twinkle for a moment, and then everything is lost to the steam.

Chapter 9.

Eli

The TV is rotated out from the wall so we can see it from the bed. The actress is blonde and young and she sings karaoke in a pink wig. I'm leaning back against the crushed velvet headboard. Jane is tucked in beneath my arm. She absentmindedly plays with my fingers. They're pruny from the pool and a long hot shower. The natural gas flames in the faux fireplace dance. They pump out just enough heat to offset the cold air coming in through the open patio door. We're watching, but we're not watching. We've both seen this movie before.

"Gawd, I love these robes," Jane says. "I don't know why, but a terry cloth robe in a hotel feels like the most luxurious thing."

"We earned them," I say.

"You earned them with your dancing," she says, "attempted dancing anyway."

"Hey! I earned it when you dragged me into the pool," I reply. "I'm sending the dry cleaning bill to you." She pokes me in the ribs. I laugh and tickle her back.

"Stop! Stop!" she says. Her breathing is fast and hoarse. She wraps her arms around me. "You know, it will be like this all the time when we live together."

"Maybe not exactly like this," I say. "We don't have robes at home."

"Not yet," Jane replies.

"Not yet," I agree. On-screen, the heroine runs through the streets of Tokyo.

"Are you sure you want to do this? Move in together?" she asks. "I know I keep asking, but you'd have to be with me all the time. You do realize that?"

I'm sure, I think. *Right?* I see us together in bed, watching movies and laughing. I see us eating dinner and climbing on the roof to watch the sunset. I see us kissing each other goodbye in the morning and drinking cocktails at night. I see the couple with their daughter at the pool. I see Jane breaking through the surface of the pool. *Am I sure? I'm sure. I'm sure that I'm sure. I think I'm sure. I am, I think.*

"Eli?" Jane says.

"Yeah. What? Sorry," I reply.

"Where did you go?" she asks. "Everything alright?"

"I'm here. I'm okay," I reply. I wrap my arm around Jane. The robe is soft against my hand. *I'm okay. If I'm with you, I'm okay.*

Jane

The cotton is soft, and I want to bury my face into Eli's chest. I lean up against him instead. My cheek rests against the fabric. The actress is lovely, and it's a good movie, but I've seen it before. She doesn't know who she is, but she thinks she knows who she wants to be. She's still at the beginning of adulthood and already questioning her choices. We see the endless future stretching out before her, even if she doesn't. I already know the momentary sadness she'll feel. I see the confusion and the joy. I've known them. For her, this is just an interlude in her youth. *To be so young,* I think. *To feel everything, every moment, so hard. I remember.*

Eli's arm is tucked in behind me. His fingertips drum a soft tune on my hip. My glass rests against his thigh. I can still taste the sweetness of the orange and sugar on my lips. I can still feel the rawness of the brandy at the back of my throat.

The actors onscreen sing karaoke—loudly, badly. They haven't yet lost whatever it is that they've found together exploring the streets late at night. I close my eyes and let my breathing relax in time with the drumming of Eli's fingertips.

"Hey, Jane?" Eli whispers.

"Hmm?" I say.

"What are you thinking about?" he asks.

"How I wish I could still be young like her. How soft my robe is, and how I want another Sidecar. I know that I don't really want one, but also, I really do," I reply. "You?"

"You remember the couple dancing with their little girl?" he asks.

"I don't think that's this movie," I reply.

"No, by the pool. Earlier," he says. The drumming stops, and he squeezes my leg. On the screen, the girl gets tucked into bed in her hotel room by an old man. *Father figure or lover? I can't remember.*

"The younger couple," I reply. "I remember."

"Yeah. Younger than us anyway," Eli replies. He is quiet for a long moment.

Oh. Where is this going, Eli?

"Everything is okay. They just popped into my head, is all," he says. "And you asked."

Oh. "Oh," I say. Eli's fingers start drumming again.

"I bet they'd send a Sidecar to the room for you," Eli says, and I smile.

Eli

Jane's breathing has slowed. Her breath pushes against my chest with a consistent rolling in, out, in, out. I gently pull my arm from the wedge of her back, and the pillows mashed up against the headboard. I roll to my left, inch-by-inch until she is sprawled across the bed, and I'm free. The mattress squeaks and expands ever so slightly as I stand. I hold my breath. She murmurs something unintelligible but doesn't wake. I exhale and pad off towards the bar.

I find a clean cocktail glass. It has a thin gold rim around the edge. I take a bottle off the shelf. The label is royal blue and wraps at an angle. The silver silhouette of the Rocky Mountains rests atop the distillery's name—Stranahan's. It's single malt. I pop the cork top and pour roughly two fingers into my glass.

I set the bottle back. The glass meets the shelf with a dull click. It's taller than the other bottles. I rotate it so the label is facing out. *Distinctive. Sleek. Someone spent some time on that design,* I think. *It should be seen.*

I step out onto the patio. My skin puckers, and my breath comes out wet. Laughter floats over from a nearby bungalow. Intermittent musical notes make their way through the courtyard from the bar. Steam rises from the mineral springs hot tub. I lean over to soak in the rising warmth. Condensation pools on my forehead. My cheeks begin to burn.

I take a sip of my whiskey. I swallow and press my tongue up against the roof of my mouth. I hang onto the spice and the sweet. It burns before fading away. *Fuck. That's good.*

I take a deep breath. The chill tickles my nose. I exhale. *In. Out. "Stay connected to the breath," she always says.* I take another sip and another. An airplane passes overhead. The red warning lights flicker as I track it across the sky. I take another sip, and it sloshes to the back of my throat faster than anticipated. I cough and convulse as the whiskey fights its way down. I try to swallow, but my eyes water and burn. My nose begins to run. *Jesus. Get it together, man.*

"What are we doing out here, Eli?" I mutter. *Apparently, you're talking to yourself now. Fuck. Get it together, you idiot. Everything is perfect right now.*

I take another sip. The whiskey tastes of brown sugar and caramel with just enough heat to slow me down. *Perfect, right now.*

The patio door slides open.

"Eli? What are you doing out here?" Jane asks.

Fuck. Figuring it all out. At least, I hope I am.

"Eli?" she says.

"Sorry. I'm here," I say. "I'm here."

Jane

Eli is gone when I wake up. My throat is dry and cracked and torn the way it always is after I drink too much. *And now, sometimes, after just a few. Getting old is for the fucking birds,* I think. *Dad always used to say that.*

I blink and try to focus on the bedside table. I momentarily hold onto the hope that a glass of water will have magically appeared while I slept, but no such luck. I roll onto my back and try to squeeze some saliva out of the walls of my mouth to wet my lips. My bladder pulses. Once I've thought about it, there is no avoiding getting up. *Shit. Here we go.*

I make slow movements, avoiding the inevitable exposure of skin to the air on the other side of the comforter. I shift my hips towards the edge of the bed, and my shoulders follow until there is nowhere else to go.

"Eli?" I say, but he doesn't answer. I slide my legs out from under and plant my feet. "Oh, damn! That's cold," I say. The words slip out as a whisper. I pull the hotel robe from the back of a chair and cinch it tight. An unrepressed shiver travels down my spine, wiggling my shoulders, breasts, and hips.

The room is dark, but a glow emanates from under the black-out curtains to the patio. I make my way past the bar and into the bathroom mostly by feel. I reach my hand around the doorframe and flick on the light in the bathroom. The beauty lights nearly blind me. As the spots dissipate from my sight, I catch my reflection in the mirror. *Holy hell! My hair! So light. So bright.*

I hadn't forgotten the dying of my hair, but seeing it still takes me aback. For the first time in my life, I've gone blonde. For the first time since I left Chicago, it is free of colored streaks. The roots haven't yet darkened at the base. The robe serves as the backdrop to the softer curls falling to my shoulders.

I struggle to reconcile the me that I've known with the woman in the mirror. That woman looks surprisingly elegant despite the late hour, eyes reddened from too many cocktails, and skin wiped free of makeup. She is a woman of a time. She is a woman who belongs at the edge of the piano, inspiring the stylings of Sammy or Frank or Dino. She is a woman who knows what she wants and gets it. *She is me. I think she is me. She is…*

Back in the bedroom, the heavy floor-to-ceiling shade at the doorway has been pulled aside. I step to the edge. I look out onto the patio. Purple and blue lights from under the bubbles create a silhouette in the shape of Eli's head. He is just visible above the edge of the hot tub. Steam obscures the clarity of my view. *Or maybe my eyes are still broken from all the booze.* I blink, blink, and wipe a grain of hardened crust from the corner of my eyelid.

The door croaks as I slide it open. The curtains rustle. Goosebumps travel up the inside of my thighs, wrap around my belly button, and cover my legs. The skin pulls and puckers along the backs of my arms. I see Eli's head tilt and turn.

"Eli?" I say. "You okay out there?"

"I'm okay," he says.

Chapter 10.

Jane

"Are you sure we have to go?" I ask.

"I'm sure," Eli replies.

"I was afraid you were going to say that," I say.

Eli nods over the car at me. He raises a hand. He holds his wave in place for a moment. "Goodbye, Wonderland. You will be missed," he says and disappears into the driver seat.

I lean back against the car. The metal is warm from the sun. It feels good pressing the heat along the length of my spine. I shade my eyes against the glare. My head starts to throb.

"Goodbye, room. Goodbye, Paul and your exquisitely crafted Sidecars. Goodbye, free mimosas and soft robes and Clyde and the boys," I say. *I will miss you always,* I think. I wave, and a couple of palm trees wave back.

Eli

The highway rises as we approach the long curve, transitioning us from the 10 onto the 62 towards Joshua Tree National Park. The blacktop disappears into successive rows of wind turbines. They split the sky. *They are the guardians of the desert—taller than tall. The propeller blades rotate slower than slow,* I think. Out the passenger window, the blades extend nearly to the ground. It isn't hard to imagine one breaking free, tearing through the sand, and crossing the highway, leaving shredded SUVs and sedans in its wake.

We're in the desert but seemingly never far from civilization. Homes with big water storage tanks out back and shade sails mounted over concrete patios come in clusters. RV's and rusty school buses in various states of disrepair are parked in sandy yards just off the roadway. The occasional snapshot-ready vacation home catches the eye. The official towns all have an auto repair garage that may or may not still be in business. Their entrances set off by piles of tires stacked near a chainlink fence. We pass colorfully painted artist outposts and country stores and sloppily painted political signs. They say *Fix 'Merica!* or *Vote for...* or *Life Begins at...*

In Morongo Valley, we pass the Hippie Chicken. Their concrete fence is painted with flowers and peace signs. Iron yard art lines the road. Actual chickens strut around the gravel parking lot. Scrawled in spray paint on a plywood sheet, an enticement says *Now offering puppies AND kittens!*

"Puppies, Eli!" says Jane. She points as we drive by.

"What about them?" I ask, feigning ignorance.

"We should stop," she says.

"Maybe on the way back," I reply and look over with a smile.

"Yeah, right," she replies. "I know that tone. You just wait. One day, you'll come home from work, and your apartment will be filled with puppies."

"Our apartment," I remind her. She smiles. She puts her hand on mine. It's soft and warm.

"Our apartment," she says.

We pass the gun club and the Tiny Pony Tavern. We stop at the Stater Brothers market to pick up firewood and fill the cooler with beer and ice. I turn down a side street. We pass through suburban Yucca Valley and head for the park entrance.

"So," says Jane, "When do we get to see the Joshua Trees?"

"Umm, well, there is one right there, and there, and there," I say, pointing them out along the road.

"Wait, what? But we're not even in the park yet," she replies.

"They don't only exist in the park, m'love," I say.

"Don't say it like I'm dumb. You're talking about those ragged fence post-looking trees with the weird bark, crooked arms, and leaf mullets that we've been driving by for like 45 minutes?" she asks.

"Yep," I reply.

"But I've seen those before. We saw them on the way into Palm Springs!" she exclaims.

"They're all over out here," I reply.

Why are we going all the way to the park if we can see the trees right here? Is there like a master Joshua Tree that we need to go see?" she asks.

"No. No master tree or anything. This trip isn't just about the trees anyway. It's bigger than that. It's about Thanksgiving and family and camping and being outside. You know, communing with nature," I reply.

"Oh," she says. "Okay, I guess."

"Are you disappointed?" I ask.

"No, I just thought there was something special about the trees in the park," she replies.

"I mean, there is. They're not just in the park, but with the way the climate is changing, they won't even be able to keep surviving out here, but, like I said, this trip isn't just about the trees," I reply.

"Yeah. Got it. Sure," Jane says.

"Geez. What's with the tone? Do you not want to be here if there isn't some special tree to see?" I ask.

"That's not it," mutters Jane.

"Then what is it? Do you want to go home?" I ask. *What the hell, Jane? What's with the attitude?*

"No. What? I want to be here," she replies.

"Are you sure?" I ask. "Because it doesn't seem like it."

"Sure," she says. "I'm sorry. I'm just tired and hungover and have the car sweats."

"It just seemed like you had a tone," I reply. *Breathe in.*

"No tone. I'm just annoyed that I'm hungover. I only had like two drinks," she says. "I'm just reconciling the drive all the way out here and thinking about the soft robes at The Wonderland."

"Just two?" I say. *Breath out.*

"I was obviously joking," she says. "So explain this to me again. Why do you come out here?"

"It's tradition. Dana collects a bunch of strays and drags us all out here into the desert. We cook up lots of food, drink a little beer, look at stars, and stare at a campfire," I say. "It's Thanksgiving."

"That's not really Thanksgiving," Jane mutters.

"No?" I say. I see her take a breath. *Shit.*

"No!" she replies. "Thanksgiving is being with family and having turkey and watching football, and if it isn't snowing, at least there is the threat of snow, and it—"

"This isn't any less Thanksgiving," I interrupt. "The basics are the same. It might not snow, but it will be cold at night. All the rest is the same. It's still eating and being with people that are standing in for the family. They just happen to change year to year. Joshua Tree is as good a place as any. Better than most."

"It's camping, and I'm sure it's fun, but it is not the same. That's all I'm saying. It isn't a real Thanksgiv—"

"Damn it, Jane! Just because it isn't your fucking tradition, that doesn't mean it can't be mine. Jesus," I snap. I see Jane recoil just slightly. I soften my tone. "I thought maybe the pre-camping fancy hotel in Palm Springs adventure could be one, a new tradition, one that is ours. That we make together."

"And it was great Eli, but you never go be with your Mom? You never wanted to get together with the whole family? Not be just—what did you call it—a stray?" Jane asks. I don't answer right away.

We turn onto the road to the West entrance. The homes get noticeably nicer. Hand-painted signs with arrows and coyotes or the trickster Kokopelli direct travelers off onto sandy driveways to their vacation rentals.

We pull up to the little hut at the gate. I show my I.D. and my Parks Pass. Park Ranger Alicia gives us a map. She smiles and waves as we pull away. Onward we go, miles and miles into the park. Rock formations begin rising around us. The Joshua Trees stretch outward from the road. They fill the desert in a near semblance of orderliness.

I'm not a stray.

Jane

Sand has blown into the road, skewing the lines between desert and blacktop. The trees begin to multiply as we go around curve after curve in the park. They stretch off in rows as if planted, and the midday sun illuminates the rock formations in the distance and boulder piles near the road. The stone shines white and casts precise shadows. The contrast between the stone and cloudless blue sky is stark.

I lean my head against the glass. The passenger window is cool, and with my eyes closed, I'm able to stave off some of the nausea. *Fucking Sidecars,* I think.

I glance over at Eli. He's focused on an unknown point out the windshield. *Fuck me. He's pissed. I'm such an asshole. Eli doesn't get angry often. I guess neither do I, so we don't have a lot of experience fighting. Fighting is a skill. Drew and I used to be so good at it.* I put my hand on his hand, and a wave of relief washes over me when he squeezes my thumb.

"Eli?" I say. "I'm sorry, but you never go home for Thanksgiving?"

"No," he says.

"Why not," I ask.

"We never really did that. Single mom, remember. She worked holiday shifts for the double pay. It made sense. I used to visit her at the diner," he replies.

"Oh, Eli, I wasn't thinking. I'm sorry," I say. "Really." *I really am an asshole.*

"For what?" he asks, but he isn't really asking. I try to answer anyway.

"I don't know, for having to not have holidays with a big family, I guess. For not feeling that love," she says. *Shut up, Jane. Please shut up.*

"I felt love," he says. Eli lets go of my hand and tightens his grip on the steering wheel until his knuckles whiten.

"That's not what I meant. I, I'm just fucking up what I'm trying to say," I reply. *Damn it, Jane. Shut up.* "Fuck," I mutter.

We pass signs for the Boy Scout Trail and Keys Ranch. After a long moment, he lets out a breath and puts his hand back on mine. I squeeze it tight as if I could pass my feelings to him through the pressure in my touch. He squeezes back, and I exhale. *I didn't even know I was holding my breath.*

"It's okay," he says, and I believe that he means it. "I never knew any different. When I was a kid, most of the time I saw her, it was there at the restaurant. It was a ten-minute walk from the front door of the school to the diner. If I wasn't sitting in a booth by 3:15, I'd run into her stomping down the street in her uniform, looking for me. She had to wear this white waitress outfit with orange sleeves and a little hat. She'd set me up with a Coke and some fries. I'd draw the other customers or sketch out the big house that we'd live in someday. I never felt ignored or unloved."

"That sounds like a hero's origin story," I say. "Maybe it is why you got into art and design."

"Maybe. Anyway, she still works a double shift on Thanksgiving weekend. It doesn't make much sense to fly home," he replies.

"I thought she was retired," I say.

"She is, but she volunteers to work the holiday so the new staff can take the day off, be with their kids if they have them," Eli says. "She couldn't afford to do that when I was little. A couple of times, I went to try to help, but it's, like, the worst time to travel."

"So you go to the desert," I reply.

"So I go to the desert," he says.

"With new friends, fellow strays, if you will, who become family," I say. I press my thumb into his palm and rotate it in a circular motion.

"Something like that," he replies. "Besides, Dana really is like my family at this point."

"It may not be traditional, but it is tradition—your tradition," I say. Eli smiles, and I smile because he does. Out the passenger window, Joshua Trees are frozen in half-hearted waves.

"And I'll see her soon, my mom," he says.

"You will?" I ask. "You're going home?" We pass the boulders at Hidden Valley Nature Trail and Cap Rock.

"She's going to come out here to visit us after Christmas. I was going to tell you when I picked you up the other day, but I saw your hair and forgot," Eli says.

"It is pretty shocking," I reply.

"No kidding. Now that we're moving in together, though, would that be okay with you? She usually stays in my room, and I sleep on the couch, but I could get her a room somewhere, too," he says. "I should probably clear that kind of thing with you now, right?"

"Eli," I say.

"Yes, Jane?" he says. His usual smile, subtle and sly, is back. I feel warmth creeping up my neck and across my cheeks.

"You are not getting her a room. I can't wait. We'll figure it out. Besides, if we're going to live together, especially at your place, we're going to have to make some changes to the decor," I say.

"Our place," he says.

"Our place," I repeat, and I smile.

"What kind of changes?" he asks.

"We need to Jane it up a little," I say.

"More Jane? I already buy the fancier toilet paper, and there is that candle," he protests.

"Consider those a downpayment on having a happy live-in girlfriend, my love," I reply. "A very small downpayment." He laughs. My stomach rumbles. I look down and press my abdomen with my palm.

"Was that you?" he asks.

"I know this is probably the wrong time to ask, but," I trail off.

"Ask what?" he says. We turn onto the gravel road leading into Ryan Campground.

"Do you think Dana will have brought mashed potatoes?" I ask, and he laughs. Ahead, Dana runs out into the gravel drive. A little cloud of dust follows her as she kicks up the sand. She waves her arms overhead and directs us into the campsite.

"I mean, if she didn't, we'll figure it out," he says.

"I love you, you know," I say, and Eli smiles. "And, I'm sorry about before."

"I know," he replies.

Chapter 11.

Jane

"Oh my god, Jane! Your hair, it looks amazing!" Dana throws her arms around me. "Is everything okay?" she whispers.

"Dana!" Eli exclaims.

"What? When a woman makes such a drastic hairstyle change, it usually means something, and platinum blonde is a choice, honey," replies Dana.

"Everything is fine, Dana," I say to reassure her. *And maybe myself,* I think. "I wanted something new. Going blonde felt like something every girl needs to do once in their life, at least once they've moved to Los Angeles, right? I decided not to fight the inevitable. I had a job interview, so I thought, *Why not now?* It was supposed to be a confidence booster."

"Well, damn. It looks so good, my confidence is boosted, too!" Dana replies. "And I bet you got the job looking like that." She pulls Eli into our hug, and he grins at me behind her back. "Come on, I'll introduce you to everyone. We're a smaller group than normal. You're the last of our motley crew of ragtag heathens to arrive this year." We follow Dana to the campfire, already burning mid-day, and she introduces us around.

"Hello," we say. "Hello."

"Hello," they say. "Hello. Hello. Hello."

"And this is Sabeen, my love, my heart, the wind beneath my wings," says Dana. She pulls her girlfriend away from a picnic table. She is as tall as Dana is short. Her lips are full, with a hint of gloss and a naturally deep shade of cranberry. A slight dimple accentuates her chin. *Her eyelashes are impossibly long.*

"It's so nice to finally meet you," Eli says. He takes her hand. "And this is my girlfriend, Jane."

"Hi," I say. Her embrace is warm and feels honest. We're strangers, but strangers who've been vouched for by friends. *Friends and lovers.*

"It's nice to meet you, too," she replies. "I've heard so much about you both. Dana lives to gossip about her closest friends."

"Hey!" says Dana.

"You know it's true," Sabeen replies.

"So do they, but that doesn't mean you go around telling everyone. Not cool, babe," Dana says. Eli and I laugh, and Sabeen smiles. "I need to keep prepping the food. I'll leave you all to get acquainted." Dana heads off towards a picnic table near the fire. Even from here, I can see a pile of vegetables and snacks and some tin-foil-covered pie tins.

"I love the pattern on your scarf," I say.

"Thanks, I don't always wear them anymore, but when my mom found out we were going camping, she sent me this one. She actually made it. The inside is lined with this warm, fleecy fabric. I don't know what it is, but I am fucking loving it," she says. She flips the edge of the hijab inside out to show me the fabric. "Seriously, feel. So soft."

"Well, it looks amazing, and I'm kind of envious," I say and touch the fabric. "Actually, I'm a lot envious. It is already colder out here than I thought. Yesterday, we were sitting by the pool drinking mimosas in the sun."

"Wait until tonight! I'll let my Mom know it was a hit, and —Hey!" she says. A soccer ball bangs against the back of her legs. A pre-tween boy wearing dark jogger sweats and a puffy coat open over a soccer jersey laughs. "This rascal is my son, Ian. Ian, meet Eli and Jane."

Eli gives me a look. *What are you trying to tell me, love? Did you know she had a kid?*

"Hi, I'm Ian," the boy says. He smiles and leans into his mom.

"Hey, Ian," says Eli, and he shakes his hand. I lean over and put mine on Sabeen's arm.

"Do you know if there is any wine?" I ask.

"I'm sure Dana has an open box somewhere. Follow me," she says, and I do.

Eli

"Hey, Ian. I'm Eli," I reply. His grip is clammy and limp but confident all the same. His hair is shaved up high over the ear. The roots are dark, but streaks of purple sweep to the side. He pulls the soccer ball over with his toe and kicks it up into his arms.

"You play for a team?" I ask.

"Umm, yeah, I play for the Kazoos. Umm, we play every Saturday…except this Saturday because, umm, because I'm here instead," he replies. "I'm a striker." He speaks in fits and starts.

"I'm sorry you'll miss your game," I say.

"It's okay," he replies.

"Well, at least it is really cool out here," I reply. Ian shrugs and drops the ball. He tries to juggle it with his foot but only gets a toe on the second attempt. I snag it before it shoots off too far. "Hey, do you want to practice your goal kicks?" I ask. His whole face expands and brightens as he smiles.

"Really?" he asks.

"Really," I say. "I used to play. C'mon, help me find a spot by the rocks where we can make a goal." Ian races ahead of me to the base of the boulders.

"Umm, here!" he shouts.

"Looks good," I say. I look over at Jane. She smiles and raises her glass. I know she'll be okay without me.

"Ready?" Ian asks. The ball flies past me and smacks against the boulder.

"Nice shot!" I say. Ian runs after the ball, which has careened past a spiky bush. I see him dribbling back around a Joshua Tree, lining up his next shot. He kicks, kicks, kicks.

Soon, we're laughing, and I'm breathing harder than I should. Joshua Tree is in the High Desert. *I'm feeling every bit of that elevation change,* I think. "Man, that sun is hot—hotter than it looks," I say.

"Yeah, yeah, but it was cold last night, like, really cold," replies Ian. "I could see my breath, and we had little heaters in our tent."

"Good to know, bud," I reply and lean back against the boulder. The rock is dimpled like a golf ball but not nearly as smooth. I feel the roughness of the stone on my back and shift to scratch an itch. "I'm going to take a little break. Okay, Ian?"

"Okay!" he says and takes off at a sprint towards the campfire, almost running into Jane on the way.

"Hey, future roomie," she says. "You looked thirsty. I brought you something."

The beer is cold, and condensation drips down the side. I hold it up to my forehead. "You are the best. Thank you," I reply.

"I'm well aware," she says, and I laugh. Jane leans up against the rock next to me. I scooch down into a wall sit, and our shoulders touch. I look over at her, and she at me.

"So this is what the world looks like from your level," I say. She laughs.

"Yeah, is it that much different from what it looks like from up there?" she asks. She raises her eyebrows towards the sky. She grins.

"The rocks seem taller," I reply.

"By about six inches or so?" she asks.

"Or so," I reply, and it is my turn to grin. *So dumb, but I love that we can play out such dumb jokes.* "The birds-eye view I normally have up there offers a perspective you shorties can only imagine." Jane laughs. She pokes me in the ribs. It's her go-to move. I crack the beer and take a big drink. The sun has started to move well into the second half of its daily run across the sky. Shadows have crept almost to where we are standing next to the boulder.

"Having fun yet?" Jane asks, and I nod.

"Yeah, but that kid was wearing me out," I say.

"To worn out to climb?" Jane asks

"Climb where?" I reply.

"Follow me," she says, and I do.

Jane

Eli follows as I scramble upward from boulder to boulder until we're near the top of the mound. We can go no further without a boost, some bouldering gear, or a functioning pair of wings. I sit on a flat spot, leaning back against the stone. Eli flops down beside me, and we look out over the valley. It's mid-afternoon, and the sun has already begun its descent towards the horizon where the Joshua Trees and sand and desert brush run into a ragged and jagged mountain range.

"I wish I had another beer to go with this view," Eli says.

"Well then, you're in luck. I brought a backup," I say, and pull another can of Mexican lager from my coat. "But you have to share."

"You're amazing," says Eli.

"You say that a lot," I reply. "I'm starting to believe it."

"Good. You should. It's true," he says. Eli cracks the can. The carbonation escapes with a hiss and a pfft. He takes a big swig. "Damn, that's good."

He offers the can to me, and I take a drink, too. The beer is sweet and bready. It finishes with a zestful nip on my tongue. "I should have grabbed a slice of lime," I say.

"We'll live," Eli replies. We stare out towards the desert, taking in the expanse. *We could be on another planet,* I think.

"So," I say.

"Yes, Jane?" he says.

"Umm, nothing, never mind," I reply. *I have something I want to say, but I don't know exactly what it is.* Down below, I can see Ian dragging his mom over to the base of the boulder and making her stand where Eli had stood, protecting the boulder goal from the thwack of a soccer goal.

"What is it?" he asks. I shake my head.

"Nothing, really. Look at all those crows circling over there," I reply.

"Don't think I don't know what you're doing," Eli replies. "If you don't want to tell me, that's okay, but I can tell it's something." He squints at me as if by staring into my eyes he can read my mind. "I can tell."

"Just looking at the crows," I say and smile.

"Ravens," he replies.

"What?" I ask.

"I think they are ravens, not crows," he says.

"How on Earth do you know that, Eli?" I ask.

"I am filled with interesting, yet nearly always useless bits of information," he replies.

"Yeah, you are," I say, and he laughs.

Eli

"They are bigger," I say. "They have a curve in the beak, and they don't *caw* like a crow. They make this super weird croaking noise. Plus, I think crows are more of a city bird —blacktop scavengers."

"That is all very interesting, but you still haven't told me how you know all that," Jane replies.

"I can't say, exactly. Maybe Wikipedia? Maybe a documentary? As I said, I'm a useless facts machine," I say.

"You're my useless facts machine," she says. I smile and take her hand.

"Yeah, I am," I say. "Look." I point across the campground. Flat stones, dozens of feet wide, lean up against another mound of oversized round boulders. The formation reaches into the sky, making the camper vans and tents below look like miniatures to be collected. At the top, a wedge with a rectangle for a base appears in stark relief against the pale blue sky.

Thousands of pounds of stone seemingly set perfectly in place, I think. The silhouette of a climber is paused near the top. Their body is a shadow against a vibrant sky. There is only the leftover light from the set sun and clouds, a fiery pink illuminated from beyond the horizon. Ropes extend above and below them—only slivers of shadow at this distance. The climber closest to the peak leans back away from the rock. A hint of sky is exposed between their torso and the stone. They shake out their arms. We watch as they begin to climb again. A gap grows between their feet and the rough edge of the mountain range.

"So what were you going to say before," I ask. "Was it about us moving in together? I'm okay looking for a new place if that is what you want, but I'm not sure we'll find a better deal than mine." Jane shakes her head.

"No, your place would be fine," she says.

"Would be?" I ask. *Oh, shit.*

"Dinner!" shouts Dana.

Chapter 12.

Eli

Color has taken over the dusk, but the horizon belongs to the darkness. Blending bands of black and blue and purple stretch into the night. Fading magenta streaks are the only remaining whisper of the day. The darkness consumes them little by little as it creeps overhead. I snap a photo to add to my collection of natural color files. *Future inspiration,* I think.

Across the fire pit, Jane is chatting with a guy wearing fur-lined everything and holding a guitar. He's not playing it, and from the way he's holding it, I'm not sure he even knows how. Occasionally, he runs his fingers across the strings. They emit a generic melody that, for a moment, overwhelms the crackle pop of the campfire.

She is wrapped in a colorful patchwork quilt that has seen more than its share of wear and tear. Her new blonde hair wraps around her chin. The teal blue wool stocking cap I bought for her is pulled low over her ears. Her eyes reflect the color and shine of the firelight. *Damn. Better than looking at the sky.*

"Hey there, friend," says Dana. She pops down into a folding camp chair next to me. "I feel like I haven't seen you in forever. Fuck, it's cold." She pulls her scarf tighter around her neck.

"At least, on the way to forever," I reply.

"How's work?" she asks.

"Good and better, but I'm traveling a lot," I reply. "I head back to the new property next week," I say. "The one north of Portland."

"That's good, right? My work is also fine. Somehow more boring since you left," she says, and I laugh.

"I'd like to say I doubt it, but," I reply.

"Uh-huh, and now that the chit-chat is out of the way, how are you and Jane?" asks Dana.

"We're moving in together," I say.

"What? Oh my god! Jane! Jane!" Dana shouts across the fire. "You're moving in together? Amazing!" Jane laughs and smiles.

"Let's hope so," she replies. Guitar guy frowns. Dana leans over and gives me an awkward seated hug. She laughs.

"Congrats, Eli. She's a keeper," she says.

"I know, but," I reply.

"You know, but what?" she asks.

"Nothing. It's nothing," I say.

"Yeah, right," Dana replies. "You forget I know you, Eli. That was definitely an unsaid something. Tell me. Tell me. Tell me! Tell—"

"Dana, umm, Dana, can I have another piece of pie," Ian interrupts. "I ate my turkey sandwich, and umm, Mom said to ask you if it was okay to cut the one on the table."

"If it's okay with your mom to eat it, its okay with me to cut it. Be careful with the knife. Okay? Hold it by the handle, and don't cut towards yourself. Like I showed you," Dana replies. "But what, Eli?"

"Nothing," I say. "Wow, it is so weird seeing you with him. You're like a mom."

"I know, right. It shocked the hell out of me, but I really like the gig so far. I'm not the real mom, though, and he doesn't call me that, obviously," she says.

"So what does he call you?" I ask.

"Dana. It is my name, you dope," she replies and slaps me on the shoulder.

"Ha freaking ha. It seems like you've got it all figured out. He does really seem to like you," I reply.

"Yeah, he does. I'm very likable. Besides, as the girlfriend, I have the easy job. I get to be the fun one who buys him soccer balls and takes him to the movies in an attempt to buy his love," she replies and laughs. I laugh, too, and we watch as Ian carefully cuts a piece of pie at the nearby picnic table.

"Sabeen is the real parent. She has to discipline him and meet with teachers and make sure he's a functioning human being, and she's just fucking, god, fucking amazing at it. How does she do it and still look like that? I'll never know, and I live with her. I *live* with her, Eli! She's a freak!" We both laugh.

She looks at Sabeen the way I look at Jane. So why am I not more excited about moving in together? If they can do it...

"I brought you a piece, too," says Ian as he hands a plate to Dana. "Do you want one, Eli?"

"Nah, I'm alright," I reply.

"Thanks, kiddo," says Dana. "Go eat your—" He's gone before she can finish the sentence. "Seems about right. So, you are, or you are not excited about moving in with Jane?"

"Excited," I say. Dana raises her eyebrows. "Really?"

"Really," I say.

"Okay. Then I have questions. One, are you going to move into your place or somewhere new, and two, why now?" she asks.

"I don't know, and...I don't know," I reply. "I mean, probably my place, and I am excited, I think. I mean, it is the next logical step, right? We've been dating for almost a year. We say *I love you,* and we mean it. We're both adults, you know? We should be past the figuring it out stages of life by now, and yeah..."

"That didn't sound that confident," she replies.

"I know," I say.

"It's okay to still be figuring it all out, you know. We're all just figuring it all out, forever and ever, until we die," she says. "You know you don't need to rush just because the calendar keeps moving forward, okay?"

"I know. Thanks for the pep talk," I say. Dana smacks me on the arm again.

"Oww!" I say. A hunk of pie is flung from her fork and lands on my sleeve. I pick it off and pop it into my mouth. "Damn, that is good pie."

"Of course it is. I made it! Let's say the two of you do move in when you get back. Then what?" Dana asks.

"What do you mean?" I ask.

"You know what I mean. Just think about about it. What happens next?" she asks.

"What do you think happens?" I ask.

"No idea. You probably get a fluffy little dog or something. I can't tell you what is right for you. I didn't know Sabeen would be right for me. Only you can decide, mon ami, but I will say, I think she's good for you. Do you remember when you took off on that road trip last year, to stalk that girl in Nebraska? Or was it Minnesota?" she says.

"I wasn't stalking her. I was going to, maybe, visit," I reply. "It was a journey of self-discovery."

"To-mato, to-mah-to," Dana replies, and I laugh.

"I remind you, I met Jane on that trip," I say.

"Yeah, I know. I thought you were crazy at the time, but it was the best thing to ever happen to you," she says. "After you met that one over there, all of a sudden, the confident, fun Eli that had been lost in his own trauma—real or imagined—started to emerge."

"The shark was real," I reply.

"I was just fucking with you. You know that," Dana says. "You came back from that trip alive, Eli. I don't know what you were before, but you came back better. So what's the hesitation we're dancing around here?"

"No hesitation, but—" I say.

"That's hesitation! But what? The kid thing?" she asks. We both look over towards Ian. His pie is already gone, and he's cutting another piece.

"We haven't talked about it," I reply. "It's just out there, hanging over us. The *live together* thing was an impulse. It's real, but I didn't think about it before I asked, and I wasn't thinking that far ahead either."

"You want them, and she doesn't," Dana says. I look over at Jane. She's smiling, and the glow of the fire reflects off her cheeks. The guitar guy has started to strum again. The notes are quiet but seem amplified as they reflect off the rocks behind us.

"Something like that, but, I mean, you know what she's been through, losing her first," I reply.

"You don't think she'll ever change her mind? Or you will? I mean, look at me. I never wanted kids, but then I met Sabeen. I know it isn't the same. Ian was part of the deal from day one, but look at me, I'm a fucking natural! I love that kid," Dana replies.

"Yeah, and as I've said, it seems as if he kind of likes you, too," I reply and smile.

"Hey, fuck you! Actually, you know what, *kind of like* is good enough for me. I'll take it," she says. "Seriously though, Eli, talk to her. Tell her what you're feeling. Old Eli would have never said anything and been miserable. You're not that guy anymore. Be the new Eli," she says, "and besides, you don't know what her answers will be unless you ask." She rests her hand on my arm. "Now, do you want some pie, or are you gonna be a little bitch?"

"Dang, Dana. Are those my only two options?" I ask, and we laugh. The fire crackles and pops and crackles and pops.

Jane

The flames keep my legs warm. I wrap a fleece blanket around my shoulders to keep the icy desert wind from tearing at me from behind. The sky has gone dark, and the group has congregated around the fire pit.

"So you're a bartender?" I ask. The guy with the guitar has been talking at me for a long time. *His name is Dennis, or is it Lennie? Shit,* I think. I look over at Eli and Dana. Her frizzy hair billows out from under her stocking cap. I'd join them, but they're deep into a conversation. *It looks serious. I'll wait a little—Denny! I think it is Denny. Maybe.*

Maybe Denny pulls himself up in his chair. His hand drops from the neck of the guitar. He puts it to his chest as if aghast at my question.

"Tending bar is what I do for money. Creating a musical experience is who *I am,*" he replies. "It is my gift to the world."

"Uh-huh," I reply. *It'd be comical if he weren't so serious.* Across the fire, Eli caresses his chin. It's a habit he's picked up as his scruff has lengthened. I can almost hear him and Dana talking. *Almost, but not quite.*

"So why don't you actually play something?" I ask. I immediately regret the snap of my tone. "I mean, do you know any good campfire tunes?" Denny runs his fingers lightly across the strings. They have a warm sound that is almost amplified as it bounces off the nearby boulders.

"I would, but my fingers are getting quite chilled," he replies.

"Right. Excuse me for a second. I'm going to grab another," I say and wiggle my camp mug.

"Could you?" he asks, but I'm already out of my chair. I pretend not to hear. At the picnic table, I put my mug under the downspout and turn the knob. The wine is deep red and splatters a bit as it hits the stainless steel. I let the mug fill until there is only enough room for my lips to rest at the edge.

Wine, wine, wine, you make me feel so fine. The words are in my head but I hear them in my mother's voice. I'm transported to a Thanksgiving long past. Family dinner is already done. The dishes have been piled up in the kitchen, and snow has begun to fall outside. We're snuggling down on the couches, on the floor, and on folding chairs I helped set up in a semi-circle so we could all be together watching the game on TV. *Wine, wine, wine, I wish I could have you all the time!*

"Would you mind?" asks Sabeen. She puts her cup down near mine, and I smile.

"It'd be my pleasure," I reply and fill her cup.

"You looked lost in thought there. I'm sorry if I've interrupted," she says.

"Don't be silly. I was just having a memory," I reply. "This is my first Thanksgiving away from my family. I think it just sort of hit me, for a moment."

"Ahh, I understand. My family is mostly in Ohio. They do a huge Thanksgiving feast. It was always really important to my parents. First generation, you know, and the turkey and stuffing and football made them feel very, very American," Sabeen says.

"Do you ever go back to visit?" I ask.

"We've always gone back, Ian and I. I'm the only one who ever left home, but this year, this year is Dana and I's first, so we negotiated. Thanksgiving is her holiday, and she'll come with us for E.D.A," she says.

"E.D.A? What's that?" I ask.

"Eid al-Fitr is the feast marking the end of Ramadan," she says. "It's in April. The whole family comes together."

"That's nice. You're a team already," I reply.

"We are," she replies. She smiles and takes a sip of her wine. "To be honest, I'm kind of glad we're here. Traveling this week is always so stressful, and this way, Ian gets to spend the holiday with his dad."

"His dad is in Los Angeles?" I ask.

"Barry is his dad," she says.

"Barry?" I ask.

"The guy with the guitar? The one you've been chatting with over by the fire," she says.

Barry! I was close.

"Oh, I didn't realize. I thought, um, I mean, I hadn't thought," I say. I stumble over my words.

"It's okay. I was still coming to grips with my identity when I met him. I always knew, but there is knowing, and there is knowing out loud," Sabeen says.

"Oh," I reply. "I'm so sorry. I shouldn't have assumed anything."

"That's okay. Anyway, Barry was my first and my last, but that was all it took," she continues. "And you know what? It was worth it. Barry can be very, ah, very L.A., but he's a good dad, and Ian is an amazing kid. He's a never-ending ball of energy, but I would never go back and change anything."

"And now you've found Dana," I say, and Sabeen smiles.

"Dana found me. She does that. She finds people, and they become part of her world. They can't help it. I was just one of those lucky ones," she says.

"What are you two talking about?" Dana interjects. She reaches around her girlfriend and hugs her. Her head pops out from under Sabeen's arm. "If you haven't noticed Jane, she's the tall, and I'm the small." Sabeen and I both laugh.

"We were talking about you, hon, always," says Sabeen, and Dana smiles.

"That's good," she replies. "The adoration of my fans is how I replenish my strength. I need some more of that adult juice. Gimme," she says, and Sabeen pours a little of the deep red liquid into Dana's mouth. Dana starts to giggle. Wine spills over her lips. "More!" she gurgles, and Sabeen and I break up too.

"You're a messy one, but I love you," Sabeen says.

"Ditto," Dana replies. "Jane, can you bring Eli one of the beers from the cooler? I promised I would, but I need to put the moves on this tall drink of beautiful."

"You're terrible," says Sabeen.

"Mom!" shouts Ian from near the fire.

Chapter 13.

Eli

It is late when we finally leave Dana and Sabeen cuddling by the fire pit. Barry aimlessly strums chords on the guitar. The winds pick up and begin to gust. We hear them being forced south from the peaks of the Sierra Nevada down into the desert. They pick up strength as they travel unabated over miles and miles of sand. Jane and I crawl into the back of the car. I've already laid the seats flat, zipped the sleeping bags together, and put out the pillows.

"You first," I say.

"Such a gentleman," Jane replies.

"Nah, just wanted to enjoy the view," I say, and she snorts. She crawls under the covers and holds the edge of the sleeping bag up for me to scramble in behind her. I pull the hatch down and shiver. *Damn. It's colder than I expected,* I think. Jane is already curled up with her back to me. I zip up the bag and shimmy over. I wrap my arm around her. I rest my hand on her forearm. She lets her body relax back into mine. She sighs.

"You okay?" I ask.

"So okay," she replies. "Just huddling around this hand warmer, trying to get back to cozy. You?"

"Mmm-hmm," I say. A little cloud poofs away from my mouth with each deep breath. We lay breathing. In. Out. In. Out, until we've unintentionally synced our rhythms and condensation begins to form on the windows.

"Do you remember the first time we slept together in here?" she whispers.

"I remember we were back-to-back," I say.

"We were," she says. "I remember thinking, *Jane, what the fuck are doing in the back of this little car with this total stranger. He could be a serial killer!*"

"That's what I was thinking, too!" I say.

"Good thing I wasn't," she says.

"Good thing," I reply. "I remember being so intimidated by you."

"By me? Why?" she says.

"Are you kidding? I was terrified! You basically accosted me. You kept badgering me and badgering me in that parking lot by the trail. The next thing I knew, you were in my car," I reply.

"And your life was never the same," she says.

"Never," I agree.

"I didn't really do that, did I?" she asks.

"Uh, yeah," I reply. "That was all you."

"I had been abandoned! Desperate times! I thought I might have to live in a small desert cave. Then there you were, my hero," she says. I feel warmth growing where her back pushes into my chest.

Hero? More like lucky bystander.

"Then it was your idea to pull over and sleep in the back of the car on the side of the road. Where were we? Still in Utah? I never would have done that. Not back then," I say.

"But you would now?" she asks.

"Sure, but only because of you. You make me stronger. You make me want to take more chances and be, I don't know, more better at life," I say.

"More better, Eli?" she says. She reaches back to poke at me, so I know she's joking.

"Watch those cold hands," I say, and she laughs. I let my hand slide under her shirt. She is warm and soft. I leave my hand to rest just below her belly button.

"Hoy! You're freezing," she exclaims.

"Not for long," I reply and laugh.

"I remember I could hear you breathing," she says, "while you slept."

"Okay, creeper," I say, and now she laughs.

"No, no! It wasn't like that. It was just…comforting," she says. My smile is lost to the darkness. I lean in to kiss the back of her head. Her hair smells of citrus and campfire and jasmine. I feel her shifting. Her hip presses into me as she rolls. Her body rotates against my arm until she's facing the roof. My hand cradles her hip.

"Hey," she says.

"Hey," I say.

She stretches her neck and kisses me. I close my eyes and feel the pressure of her lips against mine. Our breath gets pushed back and forth until she pulls away.

"I never felt unsafe with you," Jane says. She puts her hand on my face and kisses me again.

"Thank you," I reply.

"For what?" she asks.

"I'm not sure. That felt like a compliment, and the kiss wasn't bad either," I reply. Even though I can't see her, I know she's smiling.

"It was," she says. "A compliment, that is."

"It might sound kind of funny, but I never felt safe with you," I say.

"Never? That can't be a good thing," Jane replies.

"Trust me, it is. You were dangerous but in a good way. It was like I was afraid to come out of the dark cave I had been stuck in—willingly stuck in. The world was bright and good, and you were lighting the way, but, fuck, it was a scary path," I say.

"Oh," says Jane. She hugs the arm I've left resting over her.

"So yeah, I never really felt safe, not with you. Not when we slept in the back of the car that first time and not even when we were driving east those next days. Part of me was still thinking I was looking for someone else, but I knew, I fucking knew, I was being confronted by this, this force of nature," I say. I can feel my heart beat, beat, beat. Jane's fingers run up and down my forearm. "I know this isn't really breaking news," I continue. "You know I love you now, but I'm not sure you knew that even if nothing ever came of us beyond that drive, you would have changed my life."

Jane stays quiet for a long time. It is a comfortable silence. We listen to the wind coming down from the nearest mountain peaks. It picks up speed as it dips down into the valley, cuts across the desert floor, whistles around the Joshua Trees, and over boulders until it wallops against the car, causing it to sway and even shake. Finally, she curls into my chest and whispers, "Thank you. I love you too."

"Thank you," I reply, "for being dangerous." Jane squeezes my arm. I can feel her exhalations on my chest. I run my hand up, then down, and up along her hip again. My fingers curl around her waist. They stretch until they nearly reach the small of her back. I feel her hand press against my chest and work its way inside my collar and around to the back of my neck. Her lips meet mine.

"I feel it now," she says. "The danger." I smile and pull her even tighter towards me until our chests are pressed together, and her warmth and mine are the same. The wind is screaming louder and louder. Jane and I hold each other until —boom! The next gust hits the side of the car, and we sway together.

Jane

The coyotes wake me up. The sounds of their hunt bounce off the boulders. I can hear the excitement in their barks and anticipation in their yelps as they chase prey past the outer edge of the campground. I listen as the pack gets further and further away, out into the desert.

Eli snores softly. The hump of his body is illuminated by the cold blue of moonlight. Shallow breaths push the sleeping bag away from his face. He has buried himself away, but I can feel the warmth radiate from the core of his body. Through the window, I see the thick shadow above and beyond the boulders. The stone walls reflect the moonlight. The stars flicker above them. *"Hello,"* they say.

Shit. Why do I always gotta pee? I wonder. *How do I get out of here without waking Eli?* I unzip my side one zipper tooth at a time. It sounds louder than a jet engine. I cringe and look over, but there is no movement other than the bag near Eli's face pulsing out, pulling in and out again in rhythm. I swing my legs out of their cocoon, and the swish-swish of the bag cuts through the silence. Still no movement. I reach down and slip my sandals on by feel. I pull the handle on the door as slowly as possible, waiting for the clasp to unlatch. It finally clicks, and Eli groans. *Shit.* He shifts but doesn't appear to wake.

I push the door open. The cold pushes right back. The air catches in my throat as I adjust to the temperature outside. I step away from the car, and the sand kicks up under the soles of my feet. The wind gusts have calmed, and the moon is nearly full. It lights up the night like a streetlight. I don't really need my headlamp, but I think of the coyotes and flip it on anyway.

I walk down the middle of the gravel drive past the other campers asleep in their tents, their vans, their RVs. With every step, a million grains of sand, entire worlds, are crunched beneath my feet. Without the white noise cacophony of the city to act as cover, the sounds of my footsteps are the sounds of destruction itself. *I wonder how far our footsteps reverberate down into the Earth? With each step, does the weight of my toes create a wave of energy stretching and connecting me to the other side of the world?*

I open the door to the bathroom slowly and scan my lamp across the floor. *No snakes. No snakes. No snakes.* I'm safe, and as the door shuts behind me, I smile, remembering Eli as I first met him–frozen, staring at the rattler curled up in the red sand at the center of the trail. *We've come so far, Eli.*

I see a headlamp bouncing towards me as I make the return trip. The shadow of another camper gets smaller and smaller as they come close. I take comfort in the surrounding silence, knowing that I could make myself heard if needed.

"Miss Jane?" says a voice. It is reedy and small.

"Who is that?" I ask.

"It's Ian," he says. A breath I didn't know I was holding in escapes.

"Hey Ian, going out for a hike?" I ask. *So awkward.*

"Umm, no, but um, would you mind waiting here for me? I just need to, um, but then I could walk back with you?" he says. *Relax, Jane. He's just a kid. He doesn't know how weird you are.*

"Sure thing, Ian," I reply.

"Okay, thanks! Be right back," he says, and he scampers towards the porta-potty. I flip my headlamp off and stare up at the sky. Even with the brightness of the moon, the stars are more visible than they are from the roof of Eli's apartment. Each flicker is sharp and distinctive here, unobscured by the light pollution from buildings and cars and stadiums and televisions. There is no blinding neon sign from a nearby bodega forcing my pupils to constrict. A small red dot —probably a satellite—travels across the sky, cross-hatching below the soft edges of the Milky Way.

Ian comes running up behind me. His footsteps crunching, crunching, crunching.

"Miss Jane!" he says.

"Shhhh," I whisper. "People are sleeping."

"Sorry, Miss Jane. What are you looking at?" he asks. He's turned his volume down slightly.

"Just the stars," I reply.

"Do you know any constellations?" he asks.

"Not really. Do you?" I reply.

"Um, I know the Big Dipper, but I can't see it right now. Sometimes, I just make them up," he says.

"Really? You can do that?" I ask.

"Yeah, um, you just have to, um, use your imagination," he says. "See, look. That looks like a muffin."

"A muffin? Really? Where? Over there?" I ask. Ian nods as I point at random into the distance.

"Now you do one," he says.

"That kind of looks like a downward dog," I say and trace an outline around a set of stars with my finger. *Of course, that is what I see.*

"Like a dog laying down or a dog in yoga?" he asks.

"You know about yoga?" I ask.

"My soccer team does it during warm-ups before games," he replies.

Ahh, yes. L.A. kids grow up different. "That's so cool," I say. "I teach yoga."

"You do? Do you wanna do it tomorrow? We could do it up on the rocks!" Ian says, and I smile in the darkness.

"I do. Let's start walking, okay? We can find more constellations as we go," I say.

"That looks like a frog," he says.

"A frog? Really?" I reply. "A jumpy frog? Where? Those stars over there?"

"Yeah, a jumpy frog, sure. Now you do another one!" he says. I do, and he does, and I do again until he says, "Good night, Miss Jane."

"Good night, Ian," I whisper back as he disappears through the flap of a tent. Even though I feel the wind's chilled tentacles pushing through my layers and running up my legs, I lean back against the Prius. *Eli is in there.* I look up at the stars again. On, off, on, off, they quiver.

My life could have been so different. My daughter would have been almost three if…if…

I take a deep breath and try to hold back the wetness brimming at the corner of my eye. The dryness of the desert tries to pull a tear away from me, but tonight, I am stronger. *That one looks like a turtle. There is the head and the legs and the tail.*

The stars flicker on, off, on, off. "Just use your imagination," Ian had said.

"Good night, turtle," I say. *Good night, downward dog and jumpy frog. Good night, muffin.*

Chapter 14.

Eli

Sunrise in the desert is somehow as colorful, if not more, than the sunset. Purples and pinks and blues bleed from the horizon. They disappear into the pale as the sun rises in the east. I watch through the hatch window as the first rays paint the far-off mountain range. Stone and sand that will soon be bright, flat swathes of beige during the peak of today are drenched in golden dawn light dripping down over the shadows. *It isn't the same as bobbing in the waves at first light, but it is a heckuva substitute,* I think.

The inside of the sleeping bag is damp from condensation. During the night, the stocking cap disappeared from my head. I prop myself up against the back of the passenger seat to get my bearings. Jane's blonde hair is fanned out over the pillow, but her face is obscured.

As noiseless as possible, I extricate myself from our camp bed. She shifts in her bag, and a small moan emits from her mouth. She snorts, and I smile, knowing she's deep in slumber. *She can sleep through anything.*

It's brisk, but the morning is already warming. I restart the fire and get a kettle of water going on the camp stove. The shadows are crawling back from the base of the mountain ranges, and soon, the sun will be out in full. Across the gravel road, a pair of lanky gentlemen stretch their arms overhead next to an old Ford cargo van. Climbing rope is piled in the open sliding door. The closer of the gents nods, and I nod.

"Are you going hiking today?" asks Sabeen.

"Oh, shit!" I exclaim. "You scared me."

"Sorry, sorry, sorry, I thought you heard me coming," she replies.

"Not even a little, but not your fault," I say and let out the half laugh that humans do when a scare is unrealized.

"Making coffee?" she asks.

"Yeah, you want some?" I reply. She shakes her head.

"No coffee for me, but would you mind letting me steal some hot water for my tea," she asks and nods at the kettle on the stove. She pulls out a sachet of dark loose-leaf tea. "Would you mind adding it when the water is ready?"

When the kettle whistles, I brew up a half pot. I dig some enamel-dipped camp mugs out of a bin. They are blue with white speckles, just like my grandmother's dish set. I fill one with coffee and the other with hot water nearly to the brim. I add the tea and deliver it to Sabeen fireside.

"Thanks," she says.

"No problem," I reply. "That smells good. What kind of tea are you drinking?"

"This is some sort of jasmine and Darjeeling that Dana got me for my birthday. It is, ahh…well, it isn't great, but she was so excited to give it to me that I've been teaching myself to love it," she says.

"You could just teach yourself to pretend to love it," I reply, and Sabeen smiles.

"Not a bad idea," she says. "Thanks, either way. I really wanted something hot, and more importantly, I really wanted someone else to make it for me," she says.

"I'm glad this worked out so well for you," I say. Sabeen laughs and nods. She lifts the mug to her lips with both hands and takes a small sip.

"Ahh, perfecto," she says and smiles. I mime a tip of the cap.

"So," I say.

"So," she says.

"Are you and Dana going to get married?" I ask. Sabeen coughs and does a half-laugh of her own.

"Shit. You don't beat around the bush, do you?" she asks.

"Sorry. It's weird getting to know someone new. I don't know how it ever happens, and I'm not usually great at it. I thought I'd crack the ice a little bit," I reply.

"Crack it a little bit? I think you broke right through," she says.

"Well?" I ask.

"Are Dana and I going to get married?" Sabeen says. "Hmm."

"What a great question!" says Dana. "What do you think, love? Should we?" Dana puts her hands on Sabeen's shoulders from behind her chair and leans over to give her a kiss on the head.

"Are you asking?" says Sabeen.

"I thought you were the one asking," replies Dana. They both grin at each other.

"We're negotiating the terms of engagement," says Sabeen.

"You mean terms of the engagement?" I ask.

"Sure," says Dana, and they both laugh. "More coffee anywhere?"

"There is a little in the pot on the table," I reply. "This isn't the first time this has come up, is it?"

"No, no, it is not," says Sabeen.

"Nope!" Dana says at a volume too loud for the morning. The sound echoes off the rocks, and a startled raven takes off from the tangled and twisted arm of a nearby Joshua Tree.

"So, here is the thing—" starts Sabeen.

"One of us is already married," interjects Dana. "And that one of us ain't me." Sabeen rolls her eyes, and we hear the unzipping of a tent.

"Happy Thanksgiving! Is there coffee?" asks Barry.

"Can I have some pie for breakfast?" asks Ian.

"Hands off the pies!" says Dana. "The rest of those are for after dinner." She slaps at Ian's hand.

"I'll make more coffee," I say.

Jane

"I'm Steve number one," says the taller of the two.

"And I'm Steve number two," says the other. "We're climbers."

"You can just call us Steve," they say in unison.

"Hi, Steves. It's nice to meet you both," I reply.

"We smelled your coffee and realized we forgot to pack some. Any chance..." says the shorter Steve.

"We got you," Eli says. "Fresh pot, coming up."

The Steves express gratitude. *I should do the same,* I think. I slip away, out through the back of our campsite, and begin to scramble up the same boulders Eli and I sat on the day before. I find a semi-private flat space and sit cross-legged, looking out. I take a deep breath.

Feel your breath, Jane. It brings with it energy and vitality. Connect yourself down to the sand. Connect yourself upward to the sky. Reinvigorate your life force.

I hold the air in my lungs until I feel the sting. I hold it one more beat before I release.

Exhale. Toxins float away. This is a natural space. Breathe in and out again. What is left is the natural you. What is left will be.

The air pushes out my nostrils. It is hot on my upper lip. My abdomen shakes and curls as the last remaining breath is forced from my lungs. *Be grateful for this, Jane. Breathe.*

The landscape begins to blur—sand, the shaggy Joshua Trees, the pointed Yucca plant, and the violent crags on the horizon all become one. Every speckled ripple in the white stone that extends just beyond my knees shifts into a hyper-focused clarity. The undulations are so sharp they cause me to wonder what, if any, of this moment could possibly be real. A black beetle steps across the stone. Each extension of the leg comes up over the curve of his armored back. Up. Down. Up, down until he disappears beyond the lichen clinging to the stone.

Stay with this breath, Jane. In. Out. Stay with this life, Jane. Eli seemed happy kicking the ball around. Eli seemed happy, and I…

I'm shaken from my meditative breath by the croak of a raven. It is a jarring sound, loud and distinct. An alligator lizard scrambles past, and a bee buzzes close enough to make my insides flip-flop. I push the distractions away, but the moment is lost. *Shit. Alone, but never alone.* I take another deep breath.

"Miss Jane?" Ian says. "Are you doing yoga now?"

The horizon comes back into focus, and my breath escapes with a whoosh.

"Kind of," I reply. "I'm doing a meditation."

"Oh, sorry. That's, umm, like brain yoga. Can I join you?" he asks. He doesn't wait for an answer before scrambling up the boulders and falling into a cross-legged seat next to me.

"Sure, I guess. You meditate? Really?" I ask.

"They taught us at school. It is supposed to help us if we feel anxious or scared or just want to focus better," he says.

"That's amazing. We never learned any of that in school," I reply.

"Really? That's weird," he replies. "Can we start, Miss Jane?"

"Sure," I reply and smile. The pale blue behind the mountain peaks has begun to take hold, increasing in vibrance with each breath. The orange warmth of the mountainside travels further down into shadow. "Are you ready? Comfortable?" Ian nods. "Okay, breathe in! Hold."

Hold, Jane. Hold.

Chapter 15.

Eli

"Time for a praise break!" shouts the leader of a gaggle of teens careening past us down the hill. The trail has narrowed the closer we've gotten to the summit. There is barely enough room for two abreast, but the kids step over the white stones lining the trail and bunch up on either side, creating a bottleneck for those of us heading the other way.

Watch out for rattlesnakes, I think. My stomach tenses up at the thought.

"On three! Praise be! One, two, three!"

"Praise be!"

They chant as we weave through the narrow channel they leave us to pass by.

"Onward!"

A tall man with a tapered athletic build at the back of the pack smiles at us and presses the play button on the vintage-styled boombox he carries on his shoulder. "Praise be," he says. He smiles. His teeth glisten in the sunlight. Christian pop music blares from the speakers before I can respond.

We push past a few downtrodden stragglers. They wear baggy t-shirts for bands they are much too young to remember. I imagine they're cursing their parents for being forced on another youth retreat. They roll their eyes at us as a few of the more jubilant members of their group scurry back to hurry them along.

"Holy shit," says Jane. "I just had a major church camp flashback."

"You went to church camp?" I ask. "How'd I not know that?"

"There are still things you don't know about me," she replies.

"Like what?" I ask.

"Like church camp, for starters! When I was really little, I went every summer. It was a week-long sleepaway camp with hiking and canoeing and archery and Jesus. So much Jesus. He was in everything," she says, and I laugh. From the trail down below, we hear a cheer.

"Time for another praise break," I say. The path is getting steeper, and I can feel my breath coming in short huffs and shorter puffs. "So, what you're telling me this is the reason you're not a believer?"

"I believe in something, just not that," she says.

"Something? Like what?" I reply.

"Bigger, I guess. Something bigger. More connected," she says. She spreads her arms out wide and stands on her tiptoes to emphasize her point.

"I got it," I reply.

She nods. "Onward?" she asks and upward we walk.

Jane

The sign says, *Welcome to Ryan Mountain, Elevation 5,457 ft.* The paint has begun to flake away, but the letters are engraved deep into the wood. We wait in line with a few other hikers to scramble up on the a pile of rocks that mark the official summit. Eli takes my hand, and we stack them on the sign. He squeezes. His warmth feels like comfort.

"5,457 feet and about three inches," I say.

"Take a picture," he says. I step back while Eli poses with a hand on his hip, one leg forward, bent slightly, and a hand over his eyes as he takes in the magnitude of the desert.

In silhouette, his body is compact, efficient, with ridges along his calves and a slight curve leading up into his back. *Damn, Eli,* I think.

I join him at the edge of the summit. The desert below has flattened. The tree and bush and sand all take on the same plane as it leads out towards the mountains. Little flecks of purple and yellow dot the tips of scrub in the foreground. They become soft and hazy as the desert wind pushes them around.   My stomach grumbles. "That you? Apple?" he asks, and I nod. We sit on a natural stone bench and take in the expanse. The desert never seems to end. *It's like a painting. If we could see over those mountain peaks, would we just see more desert until the ocean swallowed it whole?*

The wind reminds us it is early winter, but the sun fights through to keep us warm. I pull off my coat, put it on, and pull it off again. Eli laughs. I squirt some water his way. Then we sit side-by-side, chewing slices of apple, looking out at nothing. I feel settled. *I didn't realize I was anxious.*

"It's all so big," I say. "It's hard to imagine we're only a few hours from Los Angeles."

"That's one of the reasons I love living out here. The ocean, the desert, the forests, and the mountains are all just within reach. In a month, they'll probably be opening the ski lifts just an hour or so from here," Eli replies. "Maybe sooner."

"Really?" I ask, and he nods.

"Do you think you'll be out here forever?" I ask.

"Until I can't afford it anymore," he says. "But probably even then. This is my home." We sit in silence until our snacks are gone, and we've drunk our fill of water.

"Shall we?" I ask. "To Skull Rock?" Eli nods and takes my hand.

"Onward," I say.

"Downward," he says, and I smile.

Eli

Jane is a few steps behind me on the trail as we loop out from the main road. It feels good to be leading for once, to know the way, to be sharing this place with her. I sweep my eyes back and forth across the sand, staying alert for movement. I listen for the telltale rattle warning me away from a crevice in the stones that have sloped upward away from the trail, but there is only the occasional shriek of a raptor and the hum of insects going about their day..

"How much further?" Jane asks.

"Just around the corner," I say. "Really, this time. Need a quick break?"

"No," she replies. I stop to look back. Her head is down, and she's focused on each step. She shifts her pack until it is slung across the expanse of her back between her shoulder blades. A line of sweat darkens her tank top at the edges. It pushes slightly downward, but my eyes wander north. The skin on her shoulders is smooth. The lines of her collarbone guide me to the delicate line of her neck, the curve of her chin, and to the blurry void where blonde strands hang free and loose. *Damn,* I think. *Damn.*

"Oh, shit!" Jane says. She bumps up against me. I slide my arm around her waist. "Gross. You're all sweaty."

"Should I let go?" I ask.

"Not today," she says.

"Never today," I reply, and I smile.

"Look," I say. Magenta flowers with yellow centers are open at the top of a beaver tail-shaped cactus wedged between two boulders.

"We'll have to come back in the spring," Eli replies. "The wildflowers in April are unbelievable some years. It's all yellow and pink and orange. The California poppies cover the hillsides."

"I didn't know you were such a flowerhead," I tease.

"You know me, pretty colors are my jam," he says, and I laugh.

"How much further? My legs are like jello, and I may need to, ahh, stop soon," I say. My stomach roils in agreement. *Hold on!* I think.

"Just a bit. Trust me, it was better to take the loop. It gets really busy on the campground trail to the rock," he says. "And the view is better from this side of the road. Look! See. There it is."

Eli points across the road that has finally appeared. Over the line of SUVs and tourists and scrub brush, a boulder rises from the sand. Indentations in the rock create shadowed caverns that look like eye sockets. I squint, and the crooked line of stone becomes a boxer's nose. A boulder blocks my view of the chin and what I imagine to be a ghoulish grin.

"Wow, that is really a skull," I say.

"Pretty cool, right?" says Eli. "The view is better from over here." My stomach flips and flops in agreement.

Eli

"I don't mean to rush you. I'm just feeling a little nauseous," Jane says.

"No worries. Want some water?" I ask. She shakes her head and puts her hand up against a rock to steady herself.

"I think I need to sit down for a moment," she replies and slides down to the ground.

"Okay, why don't you stay here? I'll get the car and come pick you up," I say.

"No, no, you don't have to do that," she replies. "I'm just a little dizzy. Give me a sec."

"Jane, I want to," I say. "Drink this. You're probably dehydrated. I'll be right back."

Jane

"Eli, wait," I say, but he's already jogging towards the trailhead. I watch as he cuts right at the road and disappears between a pair of boulders.

"I'm probably dehydrated," I mutter. I take a swig from the jug Eli left behind. My own jug is nearly empty in my pack. *I refilled it twice today already,* I think, *and I really gotta go.* I take another swig of the water anyway. *So I'm not dehydrated.*

I shift so my back is up against the boulder. The pebbled surface feels cool even through my shirt. I shift side-to-side. The scratch of the stone satiates an itch I didn't know I had. I sigh, enjoying the moment for its simplicity. It is short-lived. My stomach turns.

I wish I would just throw up. What the hell is wrong with me? And then I remember the last time I felt like this.

Shit.

Chapter 16.

Eli

"You're back!" Dana says.

"We're back," I reply.

"But I need you to leave again," she replies.

"What's up?" I ask.

"I have two big favors," Dana says. "One, will you go into town for some dinner supplies, and two, will you take that monster with you?" She jerks a thumb towards Ian. "The little shit ate a whole pie this morning even though I told him not to! I couldn't believe it." Ian waves.

"Umm, Jane might need to take a break, but I'll go," I reply.

"No, I'll go with," He ate a whole pie?" Jane asks.

"I did!" exclaims Ian.

"But, Jane—" I reply.

"But, nothing," she says. "I'm fine. I want to go along."

"Then it's settled!" says Dana. She claps her hands. "Here's what we need."

Jane

"Firewood, at least three bundles. It's going to be cold tonight, and a new pie. A good one. Not some store brand crap. I think they sell Julian pies at the market in town. Those are the best if they have any left. If someone else reaches for the last one, don't hesitate to hip check them into the cooler. Okay? Alright, we're gonna need…" Dana keeps listing off items and bits of advice for Eli to write down.

Thank god Dana saw the look I was shooting her. I didn't want to explain my need to head into town without Eli trying to go on my behalf, I think.

Ian chatters the entirety of the drive. Eli listens politely and chimes in when the talk turns towards surfing or soccer. I let my head rest against the window, watching as the Joshua Trees slide by. The road straightens as we get closer to town. Sand swirls in front of us, leaving mounds along blacktop and piled up in driveways. A literal tumbleweed bounces in the ditch alongside us for a moment. I close my eyes. *I'm so tired.*

"Jane," Eli says.

"Huh, what?" I ask.

"We're here," he says.

Yes, we are.

Eli

Jane blink, blink, blinks when I reach over and rest my hand on her leg.

"This is it. We're here," I say.

"I can see that," she replies.

"Do you want to stay here? Maybe you could nap in the car?" I ask.

"I need to grab something," she replies.

"I can get it," I say, but she smiles and shakes her head. *Don't push,* I think. "You okay?" Jane nods, but her smile disappears.

Jane

"I'll be right back," I say. "Ian, don't let him forget the pie."

"I'm on it, Miss Jane!" Ian replies.

"Jane?" Eli says.

"I'm fine. I'll find you," I reply, and heel turn away to avoid any further protestations. I find the pregnancy tests in that weird small town grocery aisle that houses *Feminine Products • Diapers • Kids Toys • Cat Food.*

I grab the one that claims to offer 30-second results. *You gotta love a small town grocery,* I think.

Eli

"Which one should we get, Ian? Mixed Berry or Apple?" I ask. Ian and I are standing in front of an endcap display filled with white pie boxes emblazoned with the blue and red logo of the Julian Pie Company. *As American as apple pie,* they proclaim. I'm not sure I know what that means, but the pies look fantastic.

"Umm, what if we got one of each?" he asks. "I could eat a whole one myself!"

"You already did that, Ian. Remember?" I reply.

"I could eat another," he says.

"Well then, we better get both," I say. "Can you carry them?" Ian nods emphatically. "Good. Which way do you think we'd find those bagged mashed potatoes? Jane really wanted potatoes today."

"That way?" he says. I'm not confident in his grocery mapping skills, but I have nothing to lose.

"That way it is," I reply.

"Maybe Miss Jane is over there," he says.

"Maybe she is, bud. Maybe she is," I reply.

"We should get ice cream, too," Ian replies.

Jane

"Excuse me? Excuse me, can you help me?" I ask. A very big man in a shockingly white apron turns around. He's holding a very big cleaver. He sighs, and his entire body seems to hulk inches closer to the floor.

"What can I do for you, miss?" he asks. "We have a holiday special on shaved turkey."

"Oh, I don't need any meat, but can you tell me where the bathrooms are? I've looked everywhere," I reply.

"Oh, no public bathrooms," he says and begins to turn around.

"Wait, no, but—" I say.

"Miss, if you don't need any meats, I don't need to talk to you," he replies.

What the honest fuck, I think. *Are you kidding me?*

"But there has to be a bathroom here somewhere, right? Help me out here, guy. Please," I say.

"No banos for touristas. Employees only," he says. This time he turns around.

I can feel the heat rising to meet my anxiety. I slap the test box on the counter and take a deep breath.

"Look, you shaved meat-slicing jag-off. It's an emergency. Are you going to tell me where the bathroom is, or am I going to piss all over the floor in front of your precious deli case?" I say. *That might have been out of line, Jane.*

Deli guy turns around again, and I steel myself for the inevitable shouting match.

"Look—" he says.

I point at the box on the countertop. I see the white as his eyes widen.

"Follow me," he says.

Eli

I balance the awkward stack of boxes and cans in my left arm and dig for the phone. The ringing gets exponentially louder when I finally get it out of my pocket.

"Mom?" I answer and prop the phone between my shoulder and ear. "Yeah, no. We're actually at a grocery store right now. How's the diner? Busy as always?"

Ian holds up a box of chocolate-glazed donuts. I shake my head.

"Yeah, she's around here somewhere, but not right here. I'll tell her, though," I say. "Yeah, Christmas is a go. All good....Yep...I hope so."

"What about these?" asks Ian. He's pulled a box of popsicles from a cooler.

"I don't know how we'd keep them frozen. Same as the ice cream you put back. I think we should head to the front. Jane will find us," I say. "No, Mom, that's just Dana's, ahh, it's her partner's son...I know, Mom. Maybe someday...Love you, too."

"What about these?" asks Ian. He stares wide-eyed at a small fireworks display. Can we get some?"

Jane

We push through a set of swinging doors. A whoosh of refrigerated air hits me, and I almost take a step back.

"Right there," says Deli guy.

"Thanks," I reply. "Really, I just—" He waves me off.

"Take your time," he says.

The lights turn on automatically, but only one harsh florescent over the sink is working correctly. The others are dim and blink sporadically. *It's the beginning of the end in a slasher film,* I think. I tear the box lid along a perforated path. The sticks are wrapped individually. The plastic wrap crinkles, and I shiver. *Please, no.*

The seat is cold despite the layer of toilet paper I've set down. My abs pull in tight. *Okay, Jane. You know the drill. 30 seconds. You can do this.* I set the half pink stick on the edge of the sink and count my breaths. *One-one thousand. Two-one thousand. Three…*

I stare into the metal sheet serving as a mirror in this employee bathroom. Most of my new blonde hair is tucked under a stocking cap, and for the first time in a few days, I look like myself. *Or the Jane I used to be. Only a few more seconds.*

It was only a few years ago, but it might as well have been another life entirely. I know it is only a memory but I can still feel the hot water stinging. I still hear the shouting as the blood drains away in the tub. I still hear my ex-husband's voice echoing off the tile bathroom walls and the ache in my heart that wouldn't go away. I close my eyes.

I can't do it again. Thirty-one thousand. I open my eyes and blink, blink, blink. I reach down to steady myself. The butt of my palm swipes the test into the sink. *Fuck!* I pull it out. *Is that one line? Or two? It's pink. What does that mean? Shit!*

Eli

The teller is already swiping item after item when she arrives. The machine beep, beep, beeps as the pies and potatoes pass by the scanner. Jane puts a box on the conveyor belt. I watch it run up against a six-pack of canned beer.

"Umm," I say.

"I just like to have them, and they were cheaper than at home," she says.

"Yeah, but it's already open," I reply. Beep. Beep.

"It's okay," she says. Beep. Beep. Beep.

"It's okay?" I ask. *What does that mean?* I think.

"Good luck," says the teller.

"Thanks," says Jane.

Good luck? Good luck with what?

"Miss Jane, we got you mashed potatoes!" says Ian. "But Eli said no fireworks."

Chapter 17.

Eli

"I'd like to make a toast, everyone," Barry says. He holds a bottle up over the fire. "Pass it down. Pass it around. Fill your cups with a splash or even a dollop."

"Barry, is this really necessary?" asks Sabeen.

"As necessary as the stars in the sky. As necessary as water in the sea and potholes in the Hollywood Hills! We are communing on the eve of Thanksgiving with new friends and old family. That deserves a toast," Barry replies. Sabeen nods and takes the bottle.

I try to catch Jane's eye, but she's leaning away. She puts a hand over her cup when Sabeen leans toward her, the bottle angled and ready to pour. *Fuckitty-fuck.*

The bottle is pushed into my hands. It is heavy and rectangular. It says *Reposado* on the vibrant yellow band around the neck. I shiver. *The earthquake,* I think. *I will never again drink tequila without remembering the ground shaking, without feeling the sand on my face, without feeling Jane putting her hand on mine as we raced down the coast.* I pour a healthy belt into my glass. I add a splash for good measure. *If Jane is...If we are...*

"Okay, okay, can I have your attention, everyone. Thank you. If you'll kindly raise your glasses everyone. I'm about to give the toast to end all toasts," Barry announces. Behind him, Dana rolls her eyes. She grins, and I can't help but smile back.

Barry continues, "A toast to taking a moment to slow down together. To spending this afternoon being thankful together. For surviving the wild—the wilderness—together. Please raise your glasses and take a deep, meditative breath with me." He raises his glass and gulps. The sucking of air is audible as our group steals wind from the desert.

I hear other breaths being taken and held. I realize I'm not breathing at all. I quickly suck in some air. The temperature is already dropping, and it feels cool against the back of my throat. I hold until I hear Barry release his lungs. The oxygen whooshes out.

"Let us ignore the surreality of the universe for now because for what could be the briefest of moments, it doesn't feel like we're all fucked just yet," he says.

"Jesus, Barry. That's a helluva intro to dinner," says Dana.

"Let's eat?" says Ian, and we all laugh.

"That's more like it, love. Well done," says Sabeen. She reaches over and tousles Ian's hair.

He grins and says, "Aw, Mom," but he doesn't pull away.

I glance over and catch Jane wiping a tear from her eye. I place my hand over her hand and squeeze. She squeezes back but looks away.

Jane

"Pie?" asks Sabeen. I rest a hand on my already distending belly.

"What kind?" I ask.

"Looks like Mixed Berry or Apple," she replies.

"A nearly impossible choice," I say.

"Both, then," says Sabeen. She doesn't wait for my reply before sliding the pie server under the crust.

"I think we just became best friends," I reply and smile.

"For the third time," she says. The pie goes down quickly, and I head to the picnic table that doubles as our kitchen and bar to pour myself a drink. *What the hell,* I think, and reach for the tequila bottle.

The booze is floral and light. *Is that caramel? And ginger?* It finishes with the sweetness of honey and lemon. I rotate my wrist and enjoy the weight of the ice cube as it clinks against the side of the tin mug. I know Eli is behind me before he says a word. I feel his hand slide along my hip. His arm links in underneath mine. The warmth of his breath brushes the back of my neck.

"Hey," I say.

"Is that a cocktail?" he asks.

"Yeah, it's a mule with that tequila Barry was passing around. It's good!" I say.

"Way better than the stuff we had at Duggan's after that earthquake. Do you remember how bad that shit was?" Eli asks.

"How could I forget? But after the ground nearly vibrated me into oblivion, it was doing shots with the two of you that took me the rest of the way. I'm not sure if that was really tequila or if it was gasoline," I say, and Eli laughs. I can feel his stomach pulsing against my back, and I smile.

"So, you're not—" he says.

"I'm not," I say.

"Oh," he replies.

We stand in silence, looking out into the desert. Behind us, Ian and Barry are singing a pop song cover over the strumming of a guitar.

"Hey, did you enjoy the mashed potatoes? I know they weren't home-made, but I didn't think they were half bad," says Eli.

"I forgot to try them," I reply.

"Jane!" he says.

"I know! I know!" I reply. "Thank you for getting them."

"Ian and I got those for you special," he says. He rests his chin on my shoulder. I feel the push of his cheeks as he smiles.

"I should go for a walk," I say and move his hand down to my stomach. "Will you go for a walk with me?"

"I'd go anywhere with you," Eli replies, and I smile.

Chapter 18.

Eli

"So, since we've been out here in the desert," I say, "I've been thinking."

"About alien invasions? This feels like the place to be if you want to see a UFO. Wait, were you already abducted? No one gets to probe you but me," Jane says, and I laugh.

"No, about, ahh shit, about what I want in life, I guess," I reply.

"Uh-oh, that's never good," she says.

"Sometimes it is!" I say. I jab at her, and she grabs my finger.

"Careful," she says and grins. "What about this time? What are you reflecting on now?"

"I'm not sure," I reply. My face gets hot, and I feel a knot begin to form in my stomach. Dana's words echo in my head, "*Talk to her. You won't know the answers unless you ask.*" I lean back against the boulder. I embrace the roughness of the rock pressing through the layers of fabric and scraping my skin. "I was thinking about us moving in together, and—"

"Oh," Jane says. It's almost a whisper. "You don't want to?"

"No! I mean, yes! I do. I really do," I say. I take her hand and squeeze. She squeezes back. *Don't make this harder than it has to be, you idiot.* "It's just a big step, and—"

"It is, but we're ready. Aren't we? I think we are," Jane interrupts.

"I think we are too," I reply. "I mean, we could be." Jane looks at me. She frowns and pulls her hand back into her lap.

"So what then?" she asks.

In the distance, the mountains are turning red, and the last wispy clouds in the sky are glowing pink. The Joshua Trees are well-defined shadows, and a pair of ravens croak a lullaby.

"Jane," I say.

"Eli," she says.

"Jane, the last year has been amazing. You're beautiful and smart and driven, and you push me to be better and braver. I feel like my best self when I'm in the same place with you, and still a pretty damn good version, a better version when I'm not. Even when I'm on the road, I'm trying to be someone you can be proud of," I say.

"Those all sound like good things, love," she says and puts her hand back in mine.

"They are, and the scary thing—the scariest thing—is that it isn't scary for me," I reply, "to be with you."

"Okay, weirdo. So, what is happening right now?" she asks.

"It isn't the next step I've been thinking about. Moving in together makes sense. It is the ones after that," I say.

Jane

Oh my god. He's going to propose! I think. *Oh shit. What do I do? Eli!*

"Oh my god, Eli! Are you proposing?" I blurt it out. I can't stop the words from escaping. *Shit, shit, shit! Damn it, Jane.*

Eli looks like I just dumped a bucket of cold water down his neck.

"Oh, Jane. I'm sorry, no, I—" he says, and for a moment, the world goes blank.

Jane, you fucking moron. What did you do?

"I'm sorry, that wasn't what this is, but—Jane? Jane, are you okay? Can you hear me?" Eli says. His voice breaks through my momentary fog. "Jane?" I hear the onset of panic in the timbre of his voice, and I know I have to respond.

"I'm okay," I say.

"Jane," he says. "Fuck. Are you okay? I'm so sorry. I didn't mean, I, fuck, I'm…are you okay?"

"I'm okay," I say again.

"But, you're crying," he replies.

"I am?" I ask. I run my hands under my eyes, and the collected tears run down the back of my hand. "Oh, yeah, I guess I am." I start to laugh, and then my breath gets caught in my throat. I'm laughing. I'm coughing. I'm crying, and I'm really okay, but not sure how to pull myself out of the spiral. Eli pounds on my back, and I manage to choke out the words, "I'm okay. I'm okay."

"You're okay," he repeats. "Shit. I screwed this all up."

"No, I'm sorry. I thought, um, and then I, um…It's nothing. I'm okay. I'm sorry," I say.

"Don't be sorry," Eli says. "There's nothing to be sorry for."

"I know," I reply. "I honestly don't know what came over me. You were saying all those nice things, and we're up here on this rock, the sun is setting, and then, I just, I just…" I trail off and shrug.

"You just thought I was proposing," he says and looks out over the desert. His scruff is officially a beard, and his eyelashes reach out far past his pupils. They curl just slightly. They are long slivers of darkness blocking the blurring of the magenta-hewed sky beyond the outline of his profile.

For the first time, I can see what he looks like in 5, 10, 20 years. Eli of today looks back at me, but all I see is the Eli of the future. He has distinguished wrinkles around his eyes. His chin is defined by a rugged white scruff. He smiles at me, and I wonder if he can really see me. *God, your eyelashes are so long. Men have all the luck.*

"I did, but I don't now, and I'm okay," I reply. "It's okay."

"Okay," he replies.

Eli

"What were you going say," she asks. She's staring at me, and it is hard to meet her gaze.

"Are you sure you want me to finish? We can talk later if you want," I say. *You'll never know if you don't ask her,* I think. The words are in my head, but I hear them in Dana's voice. *Shut up, Dana.*

"I told you I'm okay, Eli. I'm reversing back to when you were saying things weren't scary. Shneep shnop shmeep shmorp. Okay, go," she says.

"What was that?" I ask.

"That was me reversing things," she says. "Obviously."

"Obviously," I reply, and I smile. Jane smiles, and we are back to where we were. The knot pulses in my stomach. "I was just saying that moving in is a big step that implies other big things. Things like proposals."

"Yes, *implied* proposals are a thing. Jesus," she says and lets out an exaggerated breath. We both laugh.

"Right, well, that would be the next thing, right? Getting engaged would be the next step, traditionally, at least," I say. "I mean, I can see that for us."

"That sounds nice and not at all like an implication," Jane replies.

"Right, and then there is marriage, and then," I say. I see the look on her face, and I know that she knows what I'm going to say. It is a look that can't be explained other than to say it's like a shadow has passed through her.

"Eli—" she says, but I continue.

"Well, the last time we talked about it, you didn't want to have kids, and then today, at the store…" I say.

"You didn't looking that excited when you saw that pregnancy test box either," she replies.

"I was surprised," I say.

"Me too," she says. "I wasn't feeling great, and then I thought…but I was wrong."

"Yeah, well, it's just, look, it really seemed like being, umm, you know, wasn't something you were hoping for," I say.

"It isn't. Not now, at least. Maybe not ever," Jane says. "Probably not ever, but—"

"Oh," I say. We sit for a moment before Jane breaks the silence.

"But you do. Want them that is," she asks. "Don't you? That is what you're trying to ask me about. Isn't it?"

"Yeah, I think that I do," I say. "I know that I do."

"Oh," she says.

"Yeah," I reply.

"So this really isn't a proposal, then?" she asks. She smiles, and I shrug. Jane takes my hand. The colors of the sunset have almost disappeared. A single star, the first of the night, appears to twinkle far above.

Jane

"Ian taught me some new constellations last night," I say.

"He did? When?" Eli asks.

"It was late. I woke up and went to the bathroom. We met on the path. He showed me the jumpy frog and the muffin constellations," I say.

"The muffin?" he asks.

"Yeah, it is very obscure. Only the coolest kids know about it," I reply.

"That makes sense. You've always been the coolest kid in this relationship," Eli says, and I laugh.

"Not so much a kid anymore, though," I reply.

"Me either," he says. He puts his arm around my shoulders. I lean in as much for the feeling of closeness as the warmth of his fleece on my cheek. We sit there quietly until all the colors are gone. The last ambient glow of daylight has begun to fade.

"What if I never want what you want? What if I said, 'Sorry, Eli. Not doing it again.' Then what?" I ask.

I still feel the water draining down my shoulders. It burned as it snapped at my skin. I saw the red rivulets running towards the drain. I still feel my heart being torn out. I feel it over and over. I can't go through that again. "What if I can't ever want that? Will we be okay?"

"I guess we'll have to figure that out, at least, if we want to keep moving forward," Eli replies.

"Oh," I say. "Well, this kinda sucks." Eli nods.

"Will you at least think about it?" he asks.

"Eli," I say.

"Yes, Jane?" he replies.

"Isn't all that moving forward stuff—marriage or not, kids or not—a Future Eli and Future Jane problem?" I ask. I squeeze his hand. I run my thumb in a circle around his palm. His hands are warm, and when they close around mine, I feel safe. *Please, Eli. Say it is a Future Us problem.*

"Passing it off to Future Us sounds nice," Eli says, "but I think time has caught up to us. Future Eli and Future Jane are here now. We are them. There is only Tomorrow Eli and Tomorrow Jane still out there."

Fuck.

"Tomorrow is so soon," I reply. Eli squeezes my hand.

"I know, but I think I can take on tomorrow if I'm with you," he says.

"Me too," I reply. *I hope so.*

"We should probably get down before it is fully dark and I fall off this rock trying to get back," he says. I nod into his chest. Neither of us make a move.

Chapter 19.

Eli

"You're back!" Dana says. "Finally! The Steves are here."

"Hi! Hi! Hi!" say the Steves.

"Wait, are there three of you now?" Jane asks. She squints her eye. The left side of her face squishes in a comically confused expression.

"Technically, I'm Stephen, but Steve is fine," says the new addition to the group.

"This sonuva is a Steve, alright," says one of the other interlopers. "He's just fancy about it."

"He's as Steve as anyone who has ever Steved!" shouts Barry. "Who wants some of this wine!"

"Whoa, whoa, whoa," we all shout as he flails. Red wine splashes the stones by the fire, and Sabeen just avoids getting brained by the bottle sweeping through the air.

"Barry!" she shouts.

"He doesn't drink much," whispers Dana. "Can't handle the adult juice."

"I can see that," I reply. "I, on the other hand, could use something strong."

"How strong?" she asks.

"As strong as you've got," I reply. Dana gives me a look but nods.

"I got you," she says.

"You always do. Thank you for that," I reply. Dana rolls her eyes.

"Don't get all sappy on me now. The night has just begun," she says. "Here, this will help. It's like a balm for the soul. Hold this," she hands me one of the coffee mugs. She pours some amber liquid from an oversized bottle. A drop kicks up onto the back of my hand.

"Don't waste that!" says Jane as she passes. She leans over and kisses the back of my hand. "Salty, yet delicious. That is a big effing bottle, Dana."

"CostMart. Only forty bucks," she replies.

"Good deal!" I say.

"Hey, are you guys doing campfire shots?" asks one of the Steves.

"Not exact—" Dana begins to reply.

"I've got just the thing!" he says and scurries off.

"Oh, shit," says Stephen.

"What is he getting?" asks Jane.

"Polish," two of the Steve's say in unison.

"Oh, no," says Jane.

Jane

"We drink it back home anytime there is a celebration or a big game or it's a Monday," Stephen says. He pours the dark, purplish liquid into the stainless steel shot glasses.

"It's a Midwestern thing," says a Steve

"Basically, anytime you want to make some bad life choices," says the other Steve.

"What are you talking about?" exclaims Stephen.

"It literally says it on the side of the bottle, dude! *Made especially to the Polish taste…* Something about good fruit, umm, here it is! *We drink it while we are yelling and hugging.* That is not something a bottle of booze made for good life decisions would say," says the other Steve.

"I'm ready to make some bad decisions," says Dana.

"Me too!" shouts Barry.

"Shhh," says Sabeen. "Geez, Barry. This is a campground, not a nightclub."

"Sorry," Barry whispers. "Should I get my guitar? I should get my guitar."

The flames of the fire cast shadows on the boulders. One pours the booze, another flails around, and yet two more blend together in embrace.

"We need more vessels," says Stephen. More glassware is procured. More shots are poured. One ends up in my hand and Eli reaches over to tap his against mine.

"This is gonna be bad," I say.

"To the jumpy frog in the stars," he says and smiles.

Eli

"I love you, but fuck you and all Steves for this," Jane says. She tosses another shot of the purplish liquid back into her throat.

"Seems harsh," I reply.

"Steves, but not Stephens!" shouts Stephen.

"That was one or three too many. Dance with me?" she asks. She reaches out her hand. The fire is already dancing behind her. Clyde's words echo in my head. "*Son, when a beautiful woman asks you to dance, you dance.*" I stand, take her hand, and we begin to sway.

"So, how do you feel about my Thanksgiving now?" I ask.

"You're asking me that now?" she replies, and I laugh. "It has had its moments. Actually, it is a lot like what I'm guessing is happening back home. Dinner with family and friends. Meeting new kids you didn't know existed. Too much food. Way too much to drink. Swap out the fire for a football game on TV, and it is basically the same."

"Told you," I say.

"Except for one thing," Jane replies. "No two!"

"What's that?" I ask.

"There is very little dancing at my family Thanksgiving and not as many coyotes," she says, and I laugh. She rests her head on my shoulder, and we sway. I can feel the fire on the backs of my hands and the wind nipping at the back of my neck.

"I love you, you know," I say.

"I know," she says. "So do we really have to decide if we are Tomorrow Jane and Tomorrow you?"

"I think we do," I reply.

"Oh," she says. Her voice is muffled with her face pressed into my coat.

"Or rather, I decide, and you decide, and then we'll know," I say. "I think I have to know. I'm sorry."

"Don't be sorry," she says.

"Sure," I say, and we sway for another moment. She pulls back, and I lean so I can look into her eyes. I smile and pull a blonde strand away from her face. I tuck it behind her ear. I pull her stocking cap down to hold it in place. "Your hair, my love. Amazing." Jane laughs, and I wipe a tear from her cheek.

Jane

"Eli, are you awake?" I whisper. My voice is hoarse. I feel his body shift as he sighs. His chest retracts from my back. His belly pushes into my spine. The expelled air warms and tickles the back of my ear.

"Awake," he replies, "but only barely functioning."

You've got to ask. Do it now. Before you chicken out, I think. My self-psyche-up speech does little to stop me from shivering, more out of fear than the temperature in the back of the car. *Take a breath. In. Out. Do it, Jane.*

"I know I already asked, but if I say no tomorrow, if I say no to that final step, what does that mean? For us," I ask. "If it is just us—me and you—then what?"

"I don't really know," he replies.

"Would we break up?" I ask. Eli doesn't answer. "Eli..."

"I'm trying not to think about it until tomorrow. That is a tomorrow problem," he says.

"Oh," I say. *Tomorrow isn't future enough. I feel alone. For the first time in so long, I feel alone.*

"That's not really fair, is it?" I say.

"No," he whispers.

"So what do we do now?" I hear the shifting of the sleeping bag. I feel the weight of his arm as it rests across my torso.

"We sleep," he says.

Chapter 20.

Eli

I walk the campground loop. The stars are still out, and the moon is a matte white fifty-cent piece over the mountain range. I nod at the camp host, who is already restocking the bathrooms. Coyote tracks—a pack's worth of four-toed impressions—fill the soft sand that has settled since the evening winds pushed through. They disappear down a hard-packed trail leading off between two tweaked and twisted Joshua Trees.

The sky has started to turn once again. Pinks begin to soften the edges of the valley. I look up at the pair of ravens sitting on the boulder where Jane and I had sat the night before. They look out over their kingdom. *Without a fucking care in the world. You should be more concerned about all of this, little birds,* I think.

You should be less, I imagine they reply.

My brain begins to compile lists of things to do. The concrete, achievable goals intermingle with the internal thread that has been running since my eyes opened. *Start the fire. Heat the water. Today is tomorrow. Grind the beans. Jane. Brew the coffee. Ravens.*

The only coffee left in the bin is whole bean. I sit at the picnic table and grind away. My arm rotates in a circle, pushing and pulling the hand grinder arm until every bean has been crushed and collected into the hopper below. I twist off the cap and smell the richness of the coarse grinds.

"Good morning, coffee," I whisper. I scoop a few spoonfuls into the press pot.

The kettle whistles. I rain the hot water down on the coffee grinds. Steam and the aroma of dark chocolate and cherry and tobacco push upward. I affix the lid and imagine I'm trapping in as much flavor as possible. The latch on the hatch of the car clicks. Jane sticks her head out. Her stocking cap sits high on her head. Blonde hair falls down in waves. Her cranberry red fleece pops, and without having to think anymore, I know what I want.

I know what I want. I want Jane, but I want more. I need more. I want Jane, and I want more. More of us—a houseful of us. I know that, and I know that I don't want this to end. Not yet. Not today.

"Good morning, beautiful," she says, and I smile.

"Good morning to you, too," I reply.

"Oh, Eli, sorry. I didn't see you there. I was talking to that pot of coffee, friend," she says, and I laugh. She crawls out of the car. She wraps her arms around me. I feel her hands wandering until they find a gap near the bottom layer and come up on my chest.

"Fucking-A, Jane! Your hands are freezing," I exclaim. She giggles and presses her nose into my back.

"I know," she replies. "So is my nose and my toes and my butt."

"Your butt?" I ask.

"Yep, trust me. It's freezing," she says. "It's probably the coldest butt in all the land," she says. Her hands slide down to my hips and pull around to give me a squeeze. "Unlike yours. Yours is so hot!"

"You said it," I retort. *Get two mugs. Today is tomorrow. Pour the coffee. Tell her. You need more. Tell her.* My stomach jumps.

Jane

"Is there enough for me?" I ask, and Eli nods. He hands over his mug of coffee. It's stainless steel and dented. The steam trails behind. I wrap both my hands around the mug, willing my palms to absorb whatever heat they can into my body. I lift it and take a sip. The steam dampens my upper lip and nose.

"Whoo," I whisper and snort. A shudder rolls down my spine. The coffee is hot, too hot, and gritty, but I can feel myself relax all the same. *Breathe. It's just another morning, Jane,* I think, but I know that isn't true. *Today is tomorrow. I am Tomorrow Jane now.*

"Thanks," I say.

"No problem," he says. He pours himself a cup and takes the seat next to me. The fire is already crackling.

"Did you sleep?" I ask.

"A little," he replies. "Did you hear the coyotes? They kept waking me up."

"Oh my god, they were crazy last night. It sounded like they were right next to the car!" I say.

"They were close. I saw tracks by the bathrooms," he says. "The ones down on the other side of camp. I walked the loop just as it was getting light."

"That's wild," I say. *So dumb.*

Eli and I sit next to the fire. The store-bought wood crackles and pops. The occasional chunk of char bursts out from the metal ring onto the sand near our feet. Eli presses down on them with the rubber toe of his Chuck Taylors. He's wearing the black and white ones this morning. He crushes them into a powder, and we sit, watching.

"So—" I say.

"So—" he says, and we both laugh.

"I feel like I'm waiting on another earthquake," I say. "A bad one, like—"

"I know. Me too, but that one up north, that was a once-in-a-lifetime quake," Eli says.

"We hope," I reply. I remember. *The elk stood still for the briefest of moments. The sand gritty against my cheek. Waves of fear. Eli putting his arm around me as the ground rattled and shook.*

"No earthquakes today, my love," Eli replies. I lean over and put my face up to his. I stretch, but I can't quite reach.

"You have to meet me halfway," I say. My eyes are closed. I feel the warmth of his breath and the soft bristle of his beard before his lips finally press against mine. *You feel like home, Eli. You feel like home. Please. No earthquakes today.*

"I love you," he whispers. Tears form at the edges of my eyes. I feel the skin around my lips pull up my cheek as I try to hold them back. One escapes anyway. It's a big, slow-rolling teardrop. My neck starts to ache from stretching so far between the chairs, and I pull away. The tear is only halfway down my cheek, and I leave it there in hopes that Eli won't notice if I don't wipe it away.

"That's a movie star tear drop," he says. I nod, and he smiles. "It's too early to cry." He reaches over and wipes my cheek with his thumb.

"I know," I say, "but I couldn't stop it. I tried. I really did, but—"

"But tomorrow is today," he says. It's my turn to smile and nod.

"Tomorrow is today," I repeat. *There are no more tomorrows.*

"How's the coffee," Eli asks.

"It's good," I reply.

"You are kind. It is good enough for camp, anyway," he says, and I smile.

"Ha! I love you too, you know," I say.

"I know," he replies. He puts his hand on my knee. I can feel him brushing his fingers back and forth along the seam of my jeans. He takes a sip of coffee and stares into the fire. "I know, but you don't think you'll ever want to be more than just me and you. Do you?"

"I've already been there once, and, you know. It wrecked me. At this point in my life, this version of us, Future Us or Tomorrow Us, or whatever we are, is enough for me," I say. "This, you and me, it's what I want. That's all."

"Oh," he says.

"But it isn't the same for you. Is it?" Eli shakes his head. He stares. I see his lips quiver, and his fingers stop their strumming. I can feel his warmth through the weight of his fingertips.

"It isn't that you aren't enough, Jane," he says. "You're so much more than enough to me."

"But," I reply.

"But," he says.

"You still want, or you think you might," I say.

"I do," he says.

"And I still don't," I reply. "I can't."

"I know," he says. The fire pops.

"I mean, I know that I won't," I say. A blackened chip of wood, a sparkling orange on one end, lands in Eli's lap. He lets go of my hand to brush it away. He stares into the fire, and I examine him, taking in as much as I can. *Take it all in, Jane. Take in the eyelashes, the curl behind the ear, the taught skin where his neck meets his chest, the way his nose angles, the curve of his cheek, and the softness of his lips. This.*

"Eli," I say. "Look at me, please." I see the redness in his eyes, and it crushes my heart in the way that only an ending that matters can. I put my hand on his cheek. He smiles, and I smile.

"So, no more Tomorrow Jane. No more Tomorrow Eli," he says.

"No," I reply. "No more tomorrows.

Eli

"If it was just you and me and our five dogs," she says. I try to laugh, but nothing comes out but a creak. Jane squeezes my hand.

"So what are we saying?" I ask. *Don't say it out loud, Jane. If you don't say it, it won't be real,* I think. But she does. And it is.

"Come with me," she says, and I do. She takes my hand and, again, guides me to the rocks at the back of the campsite. She scrambles up, leading as she always does. I try to memorize her movements. She flows from step to step, finding the invisible footholds and crevices to grip. *She's always one with the world.*

"C'mon, Eli," she says from the top. Her voice bounces outwards into the desert, and I begin to scramble upward. Near the top, she reaches down to help me up. The squeeze of her hand feels familiar. *I know the weight of her touch.*

The valley floor below stretches out forever and ever, filled with Joshua Trees and coyotes running amuck and endless gaps between the long swords of the yucca plant. At the far reaches, the desert stretches outward and upward. At the horizon, the Earth reaches up for the last remaining star. It is still a barely visible white speck of dust blinking in and out above the mountain peaks, carving away at the sky.

When the enormity of the desert becomes too much, I turn my focus toward Jane. For the moment, we are just Eli and Jane. We are—one last time—together. I flash through all the colored streaks of hair, the curve of her chest in one of my t-shirts, and the strength in her legs as she climbs.

I see her as she is now. One foot forward, she looks out with a slight smile and tears coming down her face. I step behind her and wrap my arms around her waist. I bury my face into her neck. I kiss her ear. She smells of sweet pine and sleep. My forearms rest on her hips. She leans back, trusting me with the weight of her body. I clasp my hands over hers. We look out together and breathe. In. Out. In. Out.

"Look," she says, and I do.

Epilogue.

She drives out of the campground and through the shadow of the tall climbing rock. The dawn rolls out before her. She drives past rock formations and perfectly spaced Joshua Trees. The sky brightens. Splashes of color—tents in campgrounds—catch her eye.

At Hemingway Rock, she pulls over. She parks in front of the trailhead signs. They warn her to stay on the path, to watch out for rattlesnakes and tortoises. They warn against the dangers of feeding coyotes. She stares out through the trees at the looming rock face until the tears come again. She knows they will.

She doesn't wait long. They slide along her eye. She tries to hold back the wave, but they mass at the corner of the lid. The weight of them is too great. No amount of breathing or blinking will hold them back.

They drop slowly at first. The dam bends, and they push forth. Sobs rumble from deep inside. She can feel the shake in her shoulders, in the uncontrolled contractions of her core.

The tap at the window startles her. A climber with coils of rope slung over her shoulder and dozens of carabiners clipped to her belt is looking through the window. Her climbing helmet rests, unclipped, atop her head. "Hey! Are you okay?" she asks.

Jane smiles. "No, I don't think I am," she replies.

"You will be, I think," the climber says and smiles.

"I think so too," says Jane. She smiles back. "Just not today."

"Maybe tomorrow," she says.

"Maybe tomorrow," replies Jane. The climber grins and heads down the trail. Her carabiners clink out a tune. She waves when she looks back over her shoulder before hustling to catch up with her friends.

Jane shifts the car out of park and turns out onto the blacktop. The road is clear as she descends out towards the park exit. She accelerates around a long, sweeping curve, and the world expands before her.

He watches as his car pulls away. A cloud of dust kicks up as the wheels propel it out of camp and around the corner. He puts up a hand and holds it there until it disappears. He turns back to the campground. In the distance, faraway mountains rimmed with a sliver of gold from the sun rising behind him block his view of Los Angeles. The sliver grows.

He takes a deep breath. The air is dry. It burns his throat. His tears sting in his eyes. He tastes the salt at the corner of his lips as they drain away. The fire has gone down to coals. He crumples some paper into the fire pit and stacks logs cabin-style around it. It smokes but lights quickly. Flames lick at the new wood until the sticks start to blacken. They climb skyward, and he puts his hands out to catch some of the heat.

He steps back and looks up at the jumbo rocks. They tower over him. Above the base, each boulder rests atop another as if put in place by a giant building a cairn that has long since tumbled. Step close, and the mass might overwhelm. Step back, and the scale disappears into the wide range of the desert. Little yellow wildflowers poke out from crevices in the stone down near the sand. They are beauty where one might think none would exist.

A gloved hand clamps down on his shoulder, and he feels Dana sidle in beside him. He looks down and smiles.

"Hey, Eli. Jane up?" she asks. He nods. "She leave?" He nods again. "You gonna need a ride?" His lips press together in a grimace. "You okay?"

Eli closes his eyes and breathes. In. Out. When he opens them, Dana is looking up at him. "No," he says. "I'm not okay. Not today."

"Shit. I'm sorry," she says.

"For what?" he asks.

"For today," she replies, and he nods. "But you know what?"

"What?" he asks.

"There is always tomorrow," she says.

Acknowledgements.

This was a hard book to write. My wife and I were car camping for the first time in a new vehicle in Joshua Tree National Park. I had struggled to develop a fitting end for Eli and Jane for some time. The concept for this story came to me in a flash in the middle of the night. I tried to sit up, hit my head, and searched for my notepad and pen.

In the morning—in some nearly illegible scribbles with various misspelled words spanning several pages—I could see a fully formed ending. What you've just read ends much as it did in those notes. The question was, how do I get them there? How do I make it feel real that two people who love each other could call it quits?

At first, I was incredibly inspired. I wrote and wrote. When I hit a snag, I drove to Joshua Tree to camp alone. The story would come...until it didn't. I put it away and didn't return to it for months after months. I kept stacking other work so I'd have an excuse.

It took a long time, but I realized I was avoiding Eli and Jane on purpose. Finishing this book meant the end of the Eli and Jane story. There is nowhere else for them to go. It meant I couldn't spend more time with them. I couldn't guide them. I couldn't inspire more adventures.

When I finally sat down to write, I dedicated time each morning to fight with the words. They didn't flow out of my fingers without thought like they did at the beginning, but they came with pain and struggle and work. All things my characters were feeling. At one point, rereading the last chapter, I found myself crying at a picnic table outside a coffee shop.

I had written that chapter more than a year before.

I didn't change much.

I care about Eli and Jane. They aren't real people. They aren't reflections of myself or my wife or even an amalgamation of my family and friends. They are characters that I created, lived with, thought about, and have loved for nearly four years. It is hard to let them go.

Thank you for reading the first Eli and Jane novella. Thoughtful commentary from readers made me think there might be more to their story. Thank you for reading Future Eli and Future Jane. That was a more fully formed story that challenged me to continue a voice.

Finally, thank you for reading this, Tomorrow Eli and Tomorrow Jane. I had to write it—something made me keep putting words down—but you didn't have to read it (certainly not the acknowledgments). Knowing you've connected with Eli and Jane fills me with joy.

Also, thank you to my wife, who prints and reads these drafts. Living with a writer questioning his work may be one of those *I love you despite…* moments. Thank you to everyone who wrote a nice review or sent a nice comment after reading one of the books, and to everyone I've met at a markets or pop-up shop, thank you for taking a chance. Thank you for supporting writers, reading books, and generally being the best of the best of the best. Thank you.

About the Author.

Ryan Woldt writes words sometimes. He also produces and hosts the Roast! West Coast coffee podcasts. He is based out of Southern California. Ryan feels weird about writing these words in the third person. He isn't sure what he'll write next.

You can find more of his creative work online at:

www.onewildlifebooks.com • www.roastwestcoast.com

A note from the author.

"Books are uniquely portable magic."
-Stephen King

This is more true than ever before. As a kid I used books to explore the world, learn about other humans, animals, and explore all the weird corners of my imagination. Books are more than entertainment. They provide context, answers, alternatives, and guidance when it can't be found elsewhere. Support books whenever and wherever you can.

If you enjoyed this book, please consider rating and sharing your thoughts on Amazon or social media. Better yet, recommend it to a friend or pass it along to a stranger. Your willingness to share will help others find this book enabling me to write more and more words for people to read.

Thank you for supporting books, in general, and the efforts of writers everywhere.

Also Available.

Eli & Jane

Description: Eli and Jane are each searching for a new path. Eli looks out at the sea but knows something about his future is pulling him east toward home and a girl he knew in the past.

Jane's past weighs on her as she spends her days idling in her dead-end job, building the courage to confront the people and events behind her. Neither understands how to take that first step.

Independently, they determine to set off on the road in hopes that inspiration will hit. When they accidentally find each other in the desert, they realize they are not alone in their pursuit of a new life, but will they continue that life together?

Eli and Jane is a modern road trip novella about that time in life when you begin to question all the decisions you've made, and the universe steps in to help you reset, reimagine the future, and move forward in the right direction.

Future Eli & Future Jane

Description: Future Eli & Future Jane is a novel about love and finding yourself that follows our title characters as they explore their burgeoning relationship while road-tripping up the California coastline. Along the way, they explore not-so-subtle feelings for each other, come face to face with nature and natural disaster, all while acknowledging that at this stage in life, they don't know what they want from each other other than possibly a second chance at making a connection.

Their journey begins with a hectic pick-up at LAX during the holiday season. Eli and Jane make their way north through iconic coastal communities until they reach the towering redwood forests in the northernmost regions of California just in time for New Year's Eve. In this modern road trip novel, intriguing characters float in and out of the scene, helping nudge Eli and Jane towards the ultimate question: Will they, or won't they?

Join Eli and Jane on their quest for adventure, for love, for good drink, and for self-awareness. They celebrate the holidays with friends, explore canyons and hiking trails, and discover that despite their mutual attraction, there is one big question that could trip them up. While traveling along the coast and through California wine country, they strive to figure it out for themselves in the end.

Soundtrack.

This book has a soundtrack! Search for *Tomorrow Eli and Tomorrow Jane* on Spotify to hear all the songs that the author was listening to during the writing of this novel.

From the author: Music is an essential component of my process. It helps me focus. I often create playlists for writing based on the emotion I'm trying to evoke in a particular scene. The playlists for any book often balloon as I write, but I cull down to a tight 90-minute soundtrack as a nod to the 90-minute TDK blank cassette tapes that were an essential part of my childhood.

www.ingramcontent.com/pod-product-compliance
Lightning Source LLC
Chambersburg PA
CBHW051922240626
47153CB00004B/1320